The Secret Life
of Hubie Hartzel

For Sarah Sumski,
   A pretty girl with a
charming smile—
   Hope you enjoy Hubie!
   With all my best wishes,

Susan Rowan Masters
              April 28, 1990

The Secret Life of Hubie Hartzel

by Susan Rowan Masters

illustrated by
Gretchen Will Mayo

J. B. LIPPINCOTT   NEW YORK

Library of Congress Cataloging-in-Publication Data
Masters, Susan Rowan.
  The secret life of Hubie Hartzel / by Susan Rowan Masters ;
illustrated by Gretchen Will Mayo.
     p.   cm.
  Summary: Eleven-year-old Hubie Hartzel tries to cope with his many
problems including a sick cat, a crush on his art teacher, the loss
of his best friend to a girl, and the threat of the class bully who
is out to get him.
  ISBN 0-397-32399-9 : $. — ISBN 0-397-32400-6 (lib. bdg.) :
$
  [1. Schools—Fiction.   2. Family life—Fiction.   3. Bullies—
Fiction.] I. Mayo, Gretchen, ill.   II. Title.
PZ7.M423946Se   1990   89-36402
[Fic]—dc20   CIP
                                                 AC

For
Chuck,
Ted and Jon,
With love

The Secret Life of Hubie Hartzel

1

Hubie Hartzel made up his mind that very morning: he'd put up with Ralph Marruci long enough.

But there was a hitch.

It all started before class when he and his best friend, Frank Vitanza, were walking together down the hall. For the third time that week, Marruci—nobody *ever* dared call him by his first name—charged up from behind. He wedged his five-foot-four and one-hundred-twenty-pound body between Hubie and Frank, shoving them aside like swinging doors.

"Outta my way," Marruci growled.

"Hey, you stupid jerk!" Hubie called back. "What's left of your brain is coming out your geeky nose."

The hitch was that Hubie waited till Marruci was clear across the hall and practically out of earshot before telling him off. Deciding that he'd been pushed around long enough was easy. Doing something about it was the hard part.

Hubie thought over his problem all morning. Why did he have this trouble, anyway? Nobody else in his family did. That's when Hubie remembered Frank's telling him just yesterday that he was adopted. Now Hubie started to wonder about himself. Was he adopted too?

Hubie was the only one in his family with red hair that was as straight as uncooked spaghetti. It wasn't exactly red-red. But then it wasn't brown and wavy either, like the rest of his family's. When Mrs. Bunce started to talk about some stupid math test, Hubie started to draw noses. Hartzel noses.

"Hubert."

First he drew two noses that looked like Mom's and Dad's.

"Hubert."

4

Then, feeling the shape of his nose with his left hand, Hubie drew a profile of it with his right hand.

"Hubert!"

Hubie compared the three noses: Mom's, Dad's and his. The only two sort of alike were Mom's and his, because they both had small, rounded ends. Maybe I do belong, he thought. Nobody has ever said any different.

"*Hubert Hartzel!* This is the fourth time I've called your name."

Hubie jerked his head up.

Mrs. Bunce, arms folded across mountainous terrain, glared down at him. "You may be here in body," she began, and pointed a pudgy finger at him, "but your mind is a different matter." The gold ring she wore on her pinky was so huge and bright it almost blinded him.

He stared at the blotches of red moving up her neck while snickers erupted in the background.

Now he had even more to worry about as he lay sprawled on his bedroom floor trying to do long division. All the kids who failed the test, as he had, were assigned math homework tonight.

Hubie was concentrating really hard when he heard Stevie tramping down the hall toward their bedroom. Stevie was pretending to be Hulking Hero again.

Mom had bought him a shirt with snaps down the front. Stevie thought it was fun to leap into a room, rip open his shirt, growl and beat his skinny chest. He would even put on a pair of frayed, cut-off jeans. Hubie got up and kicked the door shut. Then he leaned hard against it.

"Hey, let me in!" Stevie shouted. When the door didn't budge, he added, "It's *my* bedroom too!"

Stevie is spoiled rotten, figured Hubie. When he was a baby, everybody went gooey over him. It was disgusting how they'd poke his baby rolls with their fingers and call him adorable.

Stevie kicked the door. "I'm gonna tell Mom!"

"Go right ahead," Hubie answered. "But I'll tell her that with all your fooling around I couldn't get my homework done."

Silence.

It usually took a while for anything to get past Stevie's cauliflower ears. Good, it finally got through, Hubie decided when he heard footsteps stomping away. He had enough to deal with without Stevie bugging him.

Hubie thought of his math test and the "39%" scrawled in red at the top. He had stuffed it into the wastepaper basket when Mrs. Bunce left the room for a couple of minutes. Marruci had retrieved it when Hubie's back was turned.

"Hey, everybody, take a look," Marruci had yelled, waving the paper in the air. "Hubert got a whole thirty—"

Hubie tried to grab away his paper, but he tripped and landed spread-eagle on Mrs. Bunce's desk. A stack of papers flew up, scattering all over the floor. When the click of heels sounded outside the door, Marruci darted back to his seat—and safety.

"What on earth!" Mrs. Bunce bellowed as she watched Hubie gather the papers off the floor.

"I . . . I tripped," Hubie stammered. Inside he was burning mad. Marruci had stuck it to him once again.

"You shouldn't have been out of your seat in the first place. You know the rules. I'll see *you* after school," she had added in a drill sergeant's voice.

Hubie examined the callus on his right forefinger. It's no wonder he'd got it. Making him write one hundred times "I will stay in my seat when Mrs. Bunce is out of the room" was stinky.

His stomach started to grumble. Hubie never could spend much time worrying before hunger pains took over. He headed out the door. Downstairs in the kitchen he found bananas and oranges in the fruit bowl. He wasn't allowed any of the good stuff for snacks. Like chocolate chip cookies or the rest of the apple pie Mom had shoved way back in the refrigerator.

Just as he was pulling out the pie, a loud grunt from behind made him spin around. The pie tin slipped to the floor.

"Grrr!" roared Stevie, banging his clenched fists against his bare chest.

"Get outta here!" Hubie yelled as Stevie ran out the back door. Hubie wondered if Mom had heard the racket. He tiptoed to the open doorway and listened.

"Yes, of course, Mrs. Bunce," Mom said.

His stomach tightened. Why would Mom be talking on the phone with Mrs. Bunce? And about what? So he hadn't been doing terrific work lately, but there had to be kids who were doing worse.

Boy, that apple pie would taste . . . Oh, no . . . he had almost forgotten. Hubie skidded over to where the pie lay flattened like a half-moon on the floor. Grabbing what he could, he hurried over to the garbage. That was where Mom found him.

"Hubert Claude Hartzel, what's going on here?"

"Nothin', Ma. Oh, you mean the pie. It just sort of slipped out of the frige when I, ah, opened the door." He could tell she didn't believe him.

"You know you're not supposed to eat things like that between meals. If you're hungry there is always plenty of fruit around."

He was in no mood to argue over a miserable apple or banana right now. Instead, bobbing his head, he cleaned up the mess, pulled the garbage bag out of the bin and hauled it outside. At least nobody could bug him for not taking out the garbage.

Back inside, he almost tripped over Fred Ferkle slowly heaving his hindquarters up the stairs. Picking him up, Hubie figured age was getting to Fred. After all, a sixteen-year-old cat isn't exactly at its peak.

In his bedroom, he ripped a sheet of paper out of his notebook and started to draw a boxing ring like the one at Madison Square Garden. He'd seen it on TV over at Frank's house. Mom and Dad never let him watch the fights at home. Mom always said they were a disgrace. And Dad usually said something like, "How can parents allow their kids to watch outright brutality?"

Hubie figured, What they don't know can't hurt them.

. . . "Boom Boom Hartzel is dancing around Marruci," says the announcer. "There it is, folks. Boom Boom's famous left-right combination."

Marruci tries to back off, but Hubie slams him with an uppercut. Before Marruci has a chance to recover, Hubie flattens Marruci's face with a right hook.

The announcer jumps to his feet, yelling, "Marruci is *stunned*! He can't stay on his feet much longer."

The crowd goes wild, chanting, "Boom Boom, Boom Boom, Boom Boom . . ."

"Hubie. *Hubie!* Why didn't you answer when I called?"

He looked up.

Mom was standing in the doorway. "I just wanted you to know that I have a three-o'clock appointment with Mrs. Bunce tomorrow."

When she left, Hubie crumpled up the drawing and threw it at the wastepaper basket. It missed. Taking out another sheet, he wrote over and over: "Life stinks."

2

Another rotten day, Hubie thought as he jogged through gray slush to Samuel G. Love Elementary School. Hubie pulled his knit cap down to cover his ears from a blast of icy air.

Frank was waiting for him at the corner of Wesleyan and South streets. Actually, he was prancing around like an idiot.

"What in heck are you doing?" Hubie asked as he drew closer.

"Trying to keep warm. Hey, how come you're late this morning?"

13

"Got up late," Hubie mumbled. All his moaning about a terrible stomachache hadn't stopped Mom from shoving him out the door and telling him it was probably just a little indigestion. This was no indigestion. Hubie felt knotted up inside. But to top it off, Mom had decided that Stevie looked flushed. I'm the one suffering, Hubie thought, but it's Stevie who gets to stay home.

They were halfway to school when Hubie started to shadowbox and jog in circles around Frank.

"Stop that!" Frank snapped. "You're making me dizzy."

"I'm starting a bodybuilding program. And when I'm finished—look out, Marruci! I'm going to show that creep what real muscles look like. He won't mess around with me again."

"Yeah . . . sure," Frank said. "Marruci is so big his shoes look like aircraft carriers. You're going to need more than muscles to scare this guy."

"Thanks for your confidence, pal."

"I'm just being practical."

Hubie knew Frank was right. He had never once had the nerve to even look Marruci in the eye. What good were muscles without real guts?

When Hubie and Frank got to school, news

about the substitute art teacher was being announced by the class crier, Beth Pringle. Mrs. Harrison, their regular art teacher, was taking a maternity leave. That meant she was going to have a baby. And from the way Mrs. Harrison looked, Hubie figured it could happen any minute.

"Her name is Ms. Lana Slomonsky." Hubie knew Beth was enjoying the attention because she plumped herself up like a feather pillow. Her mother was a member of the school board so Beth always knew the school news before anyone else.

Hubie noticed Frank staring at Beth. His eyes were bugging out. Sometimes—like now—Hubie wondered if Frank liked her no matter how much he claimed he didn't.

"And she begins tomorrow," added Beth.

"So big deal," said Hubie, walking over to his desk. He only hoped that Ms. Lana Slomonsky wasn't like Mrs. Clarise Harrison, whose idea of art class was to make rope wall hangings. That was okay if you liked to do that sort of thing, but Hubie liked to draw. That's what sometimes got him in trouble with Mrs. Bunce.

During the morning, Hubie tried extra hard to concentrate on his classwork—that meant no drawings—and to make sure Mrs. Bunce noticed. Maybe, he thought, she'll remember how hard I'm working when she talks with Mom later.

At lunch Marruci snuck into the cafeteria line behind Frank and lifted him two feet off the floor. Hubie saw Frank blush when some of the older girls laughed. Then in the lunchroom, when the monitor was looking the other way, Marruci grabbed Hubie's lunch bag and shot it over to Pete. When Pete threw it back, Marruci ceremoniously plopped it down in front of Hubie.

"You keep your fat, hairy paws off my lunch!" Hubie shouted.

"You're going to have to keep your voice down, young man." The cafeteria monitor wagged her finger at Hubie. "Or you'll be sent to detention after school."

"Naughty, naughty," whispered Marruci. And Pete and Marruci laughed like crazy.

If only he could even the score, Hubie thought, biting into his roast beef on pumpernickel sandwich.

His stomach started to grumble as the end of the school day drew near. By the time Hubie got

16

home he was so hungry he had to practically crawl up the back steps into the kitchen.

He had just found a piece of leftover cheesecake in the refrigerator when his sister, Brenda, sashayed through the door. She caught him before he had a chance to savor more than one mouth-watering bite.

It was just his rotten luck she wasn't where she usually hung out—mugging in front of the bathroom mirror. She was always trying different shades of lipstick and eye shadow or rearranging her hair. As if that made any difference.

"Put that back!" Brenda demanded, grabbing the cake right out of his hand. Just because she happened to have been born four years before him, she thought she could boss him around.

"Ah, come on, Bren. At least let me have that itty-bitty piece you cut off," Hubie pleaded.

Brenda hesitated. "Weeell . . . I really shouldn't," she said before handing it over. "It's bad enough having a brother who's f——"

Hubie gave her one of his long, hurt looks as he swallowed the cheesecake.

"Overweight," she added. "Anyway, it's going to be *really* embarrassing when all my friends find out *you* flunked fifth grade."

17

"Hold it! Who says I'm going to flunk?"

"Mom isn't exactly having a tête-à-tête right now with Mrs. Bunce because you're doing great work."

"What's this tête-à-tête stuff?" he asked, mimicking her voice. "You're not so hot yourself. Not with zits that look like cities on a road map all over your face."

Brenda glared at him before whirling and stalking into the living room.

She deserved it, Hubie decided, grabbing an apple and following her. It was bad enough feeling like a failure—he didn't need *her* to remind him of it.

Stevie, lying flat on his back on the couch, blended in with the white sheet under him. On the floor near his head was a pail. It was perched on top of an unused plastic garbage bag to protect the rug. "You don't look so good," Hubie told him.

Stevie moaned.

Hubie was trying to decide whether he should get close to his little brother and chance picking up what Stevie had. There were definite advantages to staying home—if you weren't too sick to enjoy

18

them. But Stevie looked so awful that Hubie decided to keep some distance.

Brenda sat cross-legged on the floor reading a book. The opening music to *The Life and Loves of Linda Lovely*—or some dumb show like that—blared on the TV. Hubie walked up to the set and switched it to another channel. Now Tom and Jerry romped across the screen.

Click, click. Back to the soap. He glanced over at Brenda. She was holding the remote control. "You've got nerve! I was here first," she said.

Hubie shrugged. "I figure a person can do one thing at a time." He flipped back to Tom and Jerry. "And you're reading."

She pressed the control. "I'm not a jerk like some people who watch stupid cartoon shows. Besides, I *can* do two things at one time if I—"

He flipped it back.

Click, click.

Mom appeared in the doorway and, without one word, calmly walked over to the TV and pulled the plug. When she turned around, Hubie could tell they had gone too far this time. "I have already spoken to both of you before about this," she began in an even voice. "From now until next Tuesday the TV is off-limits to both of you."

"Huh?" Hubie couldn't believe it. A whole week. "But Brenda wasn't even watching TV," he said.

"I was here first, Mother. And then *he* came barging in and—"

Mom held up her hands. "I don't want to hear about it." She turned and looked at Hubie, her eyes boring into his. Something more important was on her mind, but he knew it would have to wait until after supper. Mom was always saying "Suppertime should be a pleasant time."

Upstairs in his bedroom, Hubie got out a sheet of paper and began to draw the execution he knew would follow supper. He drew himself on his knees, his neck stretched over the chopping block.

. . . Hubie turns to look up and sees a black-hooded executioner looming overhead, a raised ax poised in her blubbery hand. "You may be here in body," the familiar voice says. "But your *head* is a different matter."

On the executioner's little finger, he sees a flash of gold. . . .

3

The meat loaf tasted like ground-up cardboard. Even the ketchup Hubie poured on top didn't help much. He figured Mom had already talked with Dad about her conference with Mrs. Bunce.

Fred Ferkle stumbled into the kitchen, bumping into the table leg before curling up beside Hubie's feet. Fred knew who cared most for him.

"What's with that old cat?" Brenda mumbled. She was stuffing herself with mashed potatoes. "He's been acting really weird lately. And look at his fur. He looks more like a big hairball than a cat."

"He does not!" Hubie shouted.

Mom frowned at them.

"Why did Fred walk into that table leg just now?" asked Stevie, who was slumped over a bowl of Mom's homemade chicken broth.

"Shut up, stupid," Hubie whispered, kicking Stevie in the shin. The last thing he needed to hear was Dad talking again about putting Fred away.

"Ouch! Hubie kicked me."

Mom flashed him a look that meant "cool it."

Dad scooped a hunk of meat loaf off the serving plate. "Sometimes it's best to put a sick animal out of its misery."

How could they talk like that? "You can't ever do that to Fred." Hubie flung himself to the floor where Fred lay and covered the cat with his body. *"Not ever!"*

. . . Fred Ferkle lets out a yowl. "Mental abuse," he shouts. "Talk like that would make anybody sick and miserable."

"Don't worry."

Fred points his paw at Hubie's family. "That lynch mob over there headed up by your father is ready to tighten the hangman's noose around my neck. And you say *'Don't worry'*?"

"I won't let them."

23

Fred's slitted eyes narrow.

"I swear. . . ."

"Get up, Hubie," said Dad, "and eat your supper. Look, all I meant was that sometime we might have to consider the possibility. I know this is hard on you. But after all, Fred can't be comfortable the way he is."

Hubie smoothed Fred's matted fur. Before getting back on his chair, he leaned close to Fred's ear and whispered, "You can count on me."

"Wash your hands," reminded Mom. She had a thing about cleanliness.

Everything that could go wrong *did*: TV was off-limits for a whole week; the last of Fred's lives might be cut short; and now Dad wanted to talk with Hubie—privately.

He considered going to his bedroom, throwing some clothes into his backpack and leaving for good. Then they'd be sorry. Of course he'd take Fred Ferkle along. But Hubie knew that tomorrow morning, as soon as his hunger pains became unbearable, he'd return to the scene of his misery. He hated to miss breakfast, especially if Mom was cooking blueberry pancakes and bacon, with real maple syrup.

24

Hubie trudged into the family room and plopped down on the couch opposite his father. He sat there staring at his frayed sneakers, waiting for Dad to pass judgment upon him.

"Mrs. Bunce told your mother today that you haven't been doing all your math and English homework. And yesterday you got a thirty-nine on a unit math test." He rocked back and forth a couple of times before adding, "What's the problem?"

Hubie shrugged. "Math is boring." What else could he say? Mrs. Bunce thought he was stupid. Even Brenda called him fat and a failure. Who knows, maybe his own parents would agree.

"I suppose English is boring too." Dad leaned forward. "Okay, so you're not crazy about English and math."

This time Hubie nodded.

"But do you really like fifth grade so much you'd rather spend another year there while all your friends go on?"

Rubbing his toenail against the tiny hole in his sneaker, Hubie considered the possibilities. If he stayed back, he wouldn't be in the same class with Marruci anymore. Life without Marruci wouldn't be so bad. On the other hand, he sure wished he could just beat up that creep. But even if he had the guts to try, Hubie knew Dad was dead set against fighting. "There are better ways to settle an argument," he'd say if Hubie ever brought up the subject.

Dad had told them often enough that he had been in the peace movement during the Vietnam War. Hubie remembered his exact words on the subject. He said it that often. "It's harder for a man to stand up for what he believes in and say no than it is to just go along."

"*Well?*" Dad demanded an answer.

Finally, Hubie shook his head. He wouldn't want Frank to go on to sixth grade without him.

"In that case, you'd better plan on spending more time studying and getting *all* your homework done—on time."

"I'll try harder, Dad. Honest."

"I'm glad to hear it." Dad slowly moved back in the chair. "Tell you what, Hubie. If I see you trying harder, you can have a friend sleep over twice a month."

"I'll do my homework right now," Hubie said, getting up and backing out the door. He stumbled over Fred Ferkle parked in the middle of the threshold. Picking him up, Hubie noticed how thin and bony Fred had gotten.

Upstairs, he put Fred at the bottom of his bed, where the old cat lay nestled against Hubie's bare feet. For over half an hour, Hubie worked on a map of Europe, shading in mountain ranges and putting captions beside rivers and capitals.

Suddenly he sensed something was wrong. Fred hadn't moved once in all that time. Hubie would have appreciated a lick from Fred's sandpaper tongue or a nibble on his big toe. Even if it did hurt.

"Hey, lazy, ol' Fred Ferkle, wake up." Rolling Fred over, Hubie shouted, "Holy Toledo!" Fred's eyes looked like two dull marbles. And circling the edges of his mouth was a yellowish froth. Hubie tore downstairs into the living room.

"Fred's dying, *he's dying*," Hubie wailed.

Mom put down the book she was reading. "Where is he?" she asked, and rushed upstairs behind Hubie. After she quickly examined Fred, Mom picked him up in a towel. "We'll try to make Fred as comfortable as we—"

"You sound just like Dad!" Hubie shouted. "You're going to let him die, aren't you . . . *aren't you?*" He fought back the tears.

"That's *not* what I was about to say, Hubie."

"Then you'll take him to the vet?"

"Of course we will."

Hubie gave her a hug. "I knew I could count on you, Ma."

Downstairs, Mom, still holding Fred Ferkle, stopped in front of Dad's chair. "Something is definitely wrong, Claude. I think we should get him to—"

"It's late, Gloria. I'll take him first thing tomorrow morning."

Hubie spun toward Mom and pleaded, "But if we wait till then he'll die for sure."

"Why get so upset over a sixteen-year-old hairball?" said Brenda between chomps on a carrot.

"I hate you, Brenda Hartzel! You are the meanest, rottenest—"

"That's enough from both of you!" Dad roared. Then he gave his newspaper a shake and settled back in his chair.

Hubie noticed Mom had one of her funny looks. This time she directed it at Dad. "I'd take Fred but you know how much I hate driving at night in the rain. . . ."

Folding the paper, Dad finally got up. "All right, all right. I'm going," he said as he headed for the closet. "Call Dr. Danielson's emergency number and tell them I'm on my way."

Fred looked lost in Dad's big hands. "You won't let them put Fred away, will you? *Promise* me you won't."

Dad put his hand on Hubie's shoulder. "If it means that much to you, I promise."

Later, when Dad returned, he stepped into Hubie's bedroom. Hubie was sitting up, waiting for the news. "He's going to be okay, isn't he?"

"It's pneumonia," said Dad, slowly shaking his head. "I don't think Fred's going to make it. . . . I'm sorry."

Hubie's throat closed up so he couldn't even swallow.

. . . "Thank you for coming." Hubie shakes the mourner's hand.

Another mourner steps up to the casket. Together they look at Fred Ferkle lying in his small wooden coffin. Fred's front paws are crossed over his heart.

"He looks so peaceful."

"Yes, he doesn't look at all like he suffered as much as he did."

The mourner pats Hubie's shoulder. "Now, now. Don't take it too hard," he says before moving on.

Hubie slowly shakes his head. "Why did I let Fred suffer for so long? . . ."

Reminders of Fred were everywhere. His food dish, now stowed away in the cupboard. His catnip mouse on Hubie's bed stand. And his black hairs. Even this afternoon at school Hubie had been reminded of Fred. There was a charcoal drawing of a cat taped to the art room's wall. A younger Fred Ferkle seemed to glare back at him.

"Hubert . . . Hubert Hartzel."

"Huh?" Startled, he looked up at the new art teacher, Ms. Slomonsky.

"You're supposed to raise your hand for roll call," she said, looking back at him.

Hubie nodded, noticing soft brown eyes, and chestnut hair pulled back and tied with a yellow scarf. She looked as young as the girls from the high school who came two afternoons a week to help out in the kindergarten rooms. But a lot prettier.

As Ms. Slomonsky started to read another name, a humongous spitwad sailed past Hubie and smacked against the chalkboard. It dropped, leaving a four-inch wet spot. Her face reddened. Hubie waited for her to explode like Mrs. Harrison. Instead, Ms. Slomonsky continued reading the rest of the names in a slow, steady voice. She finished and began assigning everyone seats.

"Mrs. Harrison lets us sit anywhere we want. We *never* had assigned seats," grumbled Marruci as he got up and stood beside Ms. Slomonsky, dwarfing her.

"You do now," she answered, and locked eyes with him. Finally Marruci shuffled over to the second table by the window.

When Ms. Slomonsky turned toward the chalkboard, another spitwad flew past. This time Marruci didn't miss. Turning around, Ms. Slomonsky glared at Marruci. "I only give one warning," she said, lowering her voice. "Next time you go straight to the principal's office." Then facing the board again, she wrote PERSPECTIVE in large letters. "Perspective," she began, pronouncing it slowly while looking about the room until the din quieted, "is the relation between the size of an object and its distance from the eye."

She told everyone to look out the windows at the trees and buildings. "See how everything closer appears to be a lot bigger than those things farther

31

away? Even when they're really not bigger?" Then she showed them how to draw two parallel rows of trees and a building in perspective.

On the construction paper she handed out, Hubie drew the horizon near the top, just as she had shown them. While he was drawing the two rows of trees, Ms. Slomonsky came over to his table.

"You have the idea, all right."

When she smiled at him, Hubie felt a flash of heat spread across his face. He hoped none of the guys noticed. Because there wasn't time to finish the drawing, Ms. Slomonsky assigned it for homework.

"Whoever heard of homework for art class?" Frank muttered all the way back to their regular classroom.

Hubie ignored him. He had more important things on his mind. Like the way Ms. Slomonsky brushed back a wisp of hair that kept falling across her cheek. And the way she tilted her head just a bit when she smiled at him. And . . . Oh, no. He'd almost forgotten.

Fred Ferkle could be dead, or close to it, and here he was thinking about Ms. Slomonsky. And she probably couldn't care less about him anyway.

4

Dad called Dr. Danielson's office that evening. They told him Fred was still very sick. "You know, Hubie," said Dad, his deep voice softening, "it's going to take time. Fred won't get better overnight."

When Hubie didn't hear anything more over the weekend, he decided that no news was good news. But then he wondered if Fred had died and they hadn't gotten around to telling him yet. Dr. Danielson's office was always overflowing with animals; so it seemed possible. Hubie started to worry again.

Monday dragged along as fast as a snail in over-drive. The only time Hubie came out of his stupor was in art class when Ms. Slomonsky held up his drawing to show everybody.

"That's very good," she said. "Do you draw much?"

"Yeah, I guess so. My mother is always complaining because I leave my drawings all over the house."

"Maybe what you need is an artist's sketch pad. That way you can keep track of everything."

When she smiled at him, Hubie sucked in his breath like a vacuum. Before he could think of something to say, she had moved off to talk with Stephanie. He kept hoping she'd come back. But she never did.

He was still in a pretty good mood as he raced up the back porch steps into the kitchen. Hubie had figured out different ways to convince Mom to buy him a sketch pad. She'd be home now because she had Mondays off from the office where she worked answering the phone and typing things.

"Meow."

"Holy Toledo!" Hubie stopped dead and gaped at the curled-up pile of skin and bones that lay beside the stove. "Fred Ferkle?"

"Here we thought Fred had used up all nine

lives," said Mom. "Looks like he had a spare."
She winked at Hubie.

"When did you bring him home?"

"About an hour ago."

Lifting Fred Ferkle into his arms, Hubie felt
the cat's protruding bones. "Well, at least Brenda
can't accuse you of looking like a hairball." He
rubbed his face against Fred's shaved body, and
whispered, "I should've known you'd outsmart
everybody."

"He's still very weak. We have to be careful
handling him."

"I know, Mom," Hubie answered before going
upstairs to his room.

"Hey, ol' buddy," he said, laying Fred Ferkle
on the bed. "Do you know this saying about
smarties like us?"

Then Hubie started to repeat as fast as he could,
"One smart fella, he felt smart; two smart fellas,
they felt smart; three smart fellas, they felt smart."
But he didn't get far when "Four smart fellas,
they smelled fart" tumbled out.

Hubie laughed like crazy.

Dad was in for two shocks when he got home
from work. Fred Ferkle was one. The other shock

came when Mom handed him Fred's hospital bill. He claimed Fred was getting even—by thinning out his wallet.

Brenda was the last one home because she had stayed for the rehearsal of the all-school musical. This year it was *The Sound of Music.*

True to form, when she saw Fred Ferkle, Brenda screamed, "Egads! It's practically bald."

Sometimes she was positively revolting. And Hubie told her so. Even Stevie wasn't that gross.

"Mom," said Hubie that night after supper, "could you pick up an artist's sketch pad and drawing pencil for me tomorrow?" He was clearing the table while Mom rinsed the dishes and Brenda stowed them away in the dishwasher.

"Tomorrow is really a bad day. I have to stop at the Rug Shop by three o'clock to pick up the kitchen carpet samples. And right after that Brenda has her doctor's appointment. I'll get it next—"

"Ah, come on, Mom. I really *need* the pad before then. It's for my art project." Then he laid it on heavy with the same sad look Stevie always used to get his way. It usually worked when he wanted something bad enough. And if Mom had time to take yucky Brenda to the skin doctor, she could do one small thing for him. "Pleeese?"

"Well . . . maybe I'd have time to stop before picking up Brenda. I suppose it's not that much out of the way."

"Hey, I don't want to be late for my doctor's appointment," Brenda butted in.

Turning his back to her and facing Mom, Hubie pleaded, "It's really important to me. Will you promise?"

"Okay," she said, and held up three fingers on her right hand. "On an ex-Brownie's honor, I promise."

Hubie laughed. "You were a Brownie?"

"What's so funny? Mothers were kids at one time."

"Nothin'." He just couldn't picture his own mother a chocolate cupcake. Back in third grade that's what all the guys called Brownies.

The next day at school Hubie had a hard time concentrating on math. Whenever he thought of his sketch pad, his drawing fingers would itch. Hubie felt he had to draw something.

It was the end of the day and Mrs. Bunce, standing near the doorway, was reminding everybody— just like she always did—"Your ticket home is a neat, completed math paper."

He tore a sheet out of his notebook and started to draw Mrs. Bunce. The classroom became a prison with bars at the windows. And blocking the door to freedom was Mrs. Bunce in full uniform. A ring dripping with keys hung from her quadruple neck. A fleshy hand with a huge gold ring on its pinky pointed at him. Above her he wrote: "Your math or your life."

Hubie was putting on the finishing touches when he sensed someone behind him. He leaned over his desk, trying to cover the drawing as much as he could. But before he had a chance to see who it was, a hand reached out.

Marruci's face closed in on Hubie's as they clung to opposite ends of the paper. "You'd better let go," Hubie demanded.

"Sure." Marruci flashed a row of buck teeth. "But you'd better get rid of that obscene picture before Mrs. Bunce sees it." Marruci had a built-in megaphone. Hubie figured he stored it in his enormous Adam's apple.

Marruci got Mrs. Bunce's attention, all right.

Hubie saw her antenna rise three feet as she turned and stared at them.

"What's all the commotion back there?" she demanded, pushing horn-rimmed glasses up Mount Everest.

Hubie wadded up the drawing and shoved it into his desk. Then slowly he slid his math paper out from under the book and picked up a pencil.

"It would help if you were on the correct page, Hubert." Mrs. Bunce stood, arms crossed, peering down at his paper.

He focused on the page number—187. What page was he supposed to be on? Hubie wondered, trying to remember. "Ah . . . I was . . . reviewing."

"I suggest you finish page 184 first before reviewing ahead of yourself."

Ignoring the snickering in the background, Mrs. Bunce swung toward Marruci, who was slouched in his chair with one leg draped over his desk.

Marruci slowly lifted his leg off the desk. His western boot hit the tile floor with a thud.

Mrs. Bunce told Marruci that his work was as sloppy as his manners. "And while you're sitting up properly," she added, "copy your math over neatly."

When Mrs. Bunce returned to the far side of the room, Hubie whispered, "Hey, Marruci."

Marruci looked up, scowling.

Hubie gave him the finger.

Marruci hissed, "I'll get you for that, nerd!"

He was still working when Hubie got up to leave.

Since Brenda and Stevie had left with Mom, Hubie opened the back door with the extra key that hung on a nail in the garage. He went straight for the corner table in the front hall where everything got dumped, like mail and, he hoped, his pad.

Nothing!

Some of the mail had been opened. That meant Mom had come inside to pick up Brenda and Stevie. So she could've put his pad right here, just like she had promised.

"How could she forget?" he yelled. The sound, bouncing off the walls, echoed through the empty house. "I can't even depend on my own mother!"

Fred Ferkle, who had been napping under the table, stretched his long, thin body. He came out and rubbed up against Hubie's leg. "Meow."

"It's got nothing to do with you, ol' buddy,"

Hubie said, scratching under Fred's whiskery chin. Then tramping upstairs to his bedroom, Hubie shoved the door shut with the back of his foot and jumped onto the bed. At least he had privacy.

Hubie turned his stereo to ROCK 109. After punching his pillow into a ball and wrapping his arms around it, he pressed his chin into its softness and listened to Mad Morgan and the Three Zees. The stand under the stereo trembled with each beat.

. . ."In just a moment we will hear the top song on the charts." Pausing, the announcer lowers his voice. "It was a hard life for this young singer before he began his career. He endured misery and hardship. No one cared. But those early years didn't stop him. After leaving home at the tender age of eleven, he went on to become the greatest rock singer of all time.

"And now here's Hubie Hartzel with his biggest hit: 'Revenge' . . ."

He must have dozed off, because the next thing he heard was Mom calling from the bottom of the stairs. "Hubie, *please* turn down your radio."

He flipped the switch off and headed downstairs, where loud voices were filtering up from the basement. Fred, stretching as he got up, followed.

In the laundry room, Mom was stuffing towels into the washing machine. Only it looked like she was stuffing live ammo into a machine gun. Something was bugging her. He figured it had to be Brenda.

"I still don't see why *I* have to be home by eleven when nobody else has to," Brenda argued. "It's embarrassing, downright embarrassing!" Shoving her clenched hands onto her hips, she added, "You and Daddy treat me just like a . . . a child."

Hubie expected something even more melodramatic to happen next. Ever since Brenda had been picked for that bit part in this year's school musical she had dedicated her life to "the theater," as she put it.

"Mom," Hubie said, trying to wedge in a few words of his own.

"Reaching the ripe old age of fifteen does *not* make you an adult. Your father and I allow you as much freedom as we think you can handle."

"Freedom!" Brenda screeched. "What freedom?" Her face was beginning to match the color of the red sweater she was wearing.

Hubie tried again. Only louder this time. "Mom . . . I—"

"Not now, Hubie . . . please!"

"Yeah, don't butt in on other people's discussions," Brenda shouted.

"Some discussion!" he snapped.

Mom gave them the let's-cool-it look. "We'll talk later."

He started to say something but changed his mind when he saw Mom's eyes narrow. Scrambling up the basement stairs, Hubie paused on the landing. "You promised you'd get my sketch pad. *You promised!*"

Hubie didn't hear what she said because he closed the door hard. But not hard enough to make her angry about that too. Sometimes, like now, he wondered if it was really Brenda and Stevie whom Mom and Dad cared most about.

Picking up Fred, Hubie carried him back to his room.

5

Motor Mouth Stevie was sitting on the floor putting a puzzle together. He revved up as soon as Hubie walked in.

Hubie was in no mood to listen. "You'd better get to your side of the room," he ordered, and put Fred down on the oval rug beside his bed. When Stevie didn't budge, he added, *"Now!"*

"But I don't want to bust up my puzzle."

"Can't you figure *anything* out?" Hubie shoved the pieces that were already together to the other side of the room while Stevie carried over the rest of the puzzle in the box it came in.

45

"Know what?" Stevie asked, sitting back down. "When I'm all done this is going to be a map of the United States." He held up a blue piece of ocean and turned it in his hands as he examined it closely. "Now where does this go? Hmm. I'll bet it goes . . . right . . ." The ocean slid into place. "*Here!* Oh boy, is this a lot of—"

"*Either shut your trap or get lost,*" Hubie hollered.

Stevie jumped up and, kicking the puzzle hard so that the pieces flew in every direction, ran out of the room.

When Mom came up to apologize, Hubie rolled over, giving her his back. She had *promised*. "When Stevie or Brenda ask for something," he said, mumbling into the pillow, "you always remember."

He even refused to come down for supper. Hubie wasn't about to give in. He wanted Mom to feel miserable too. What if he *was* adopted like Frank? Maybe Mom and Dad just hadn't gotten around to telling him yet.

. . ."Hubert, we have something to tell you." His parents stand in the open doorway.

Oh, no. This is it. They're going to do it. They're really going to do it.

His father puts his hand on Hubie's shoulder.

47

"You're . . . I can't tell him, Gloria," he says, turning away.

"I'm *what?*" Hubie demands.

Finally Dad answers. "Adopted . . ."

That night after Stevie had fallen asleep, Hubie heard his bedroom door creak open and then close. He sat up. Something in front of the door caught his eye. Turning on the bed-stand lamp, he padded over and picked up a brown paper bag. Inside was a sketch pad and art pencil, along with a note from Mom.

"Dear Hubie, a promise is a promise." It was signed, "An ex-Brownie. P.S. Your great-grandfather Stevenson liked to draw and paint. In some ways you remind me of him."

Pressing the pad close to him, Hubie thought about this great-grandfather he'd never seen. Did he have red hair too? Hubie wondered. Now that his hunger strike was over, he snuck downstairs for something to eat. But all he found was a lousy piece of leftover chicken and a couple of apples in the fruit bowl. Chicken might be his least favorite food, but it sure beat starvation, he decided, and took a bite.

* * *

The next morning Hubie got up before Brenda and Stevie. Mom called his early rising "an event that normally happens once a year—Christmas morning."

He had just started to eat when Her Royal Highness swept into the kitchen and sat down. "Pass the milk," she ordered. When the milk stayed put, Brenda finally added, "Pleeeese." She ate in silence.

Brenda wasn't the only one acting weird. Stevie, still angry with Hubie for yelling at him last night, was sitting with his arms crossed and his lower lip puckered out. "It looks yucky," he mumbled into his bowl of cereal.

"We don't have time for any nonsense," said Mom. "Now eat!"

Picking up his spoon, Stevie slapped the rounded end into his Rice Krunchies, spraying milk all over the table.

"Only babies act like that," Mom told Stevie, and sponged off the mess. Then Dad took away his spoon and cereal bowl.

For once they were seeing Stevie for what he was—a spoiled creep. It warmed Hubie's heart.

Hungrily he dug into his bowl of Monster Chocula. "You can't beat Monster Chocula's gigantic cocoa flakes," he silently read off the front panel of the cereal box.

"His loud munching sounds like an invading army of carpenter ants," Brenda piped up, boring into Hubie with her beady eyes.

Boy, did she have it in for him. And he hadn't even done anything to her . . . yet. "Oh yeah?" Hubie countered. "At least *I* don't—"

"Hold it," said Dad, getting up. "It's too early in the morning to start arguing." Grabbing his coat, he paused beside the door. "Keep the peace, my little chickadees. Hee, hee, hee." Then he hightailed it out the door.

After Dad and Brenda left, Hubie decided to ask about his great-grandfather. "Mom," he began, looking over the box of Monster Chocula, "tell me about my great-grandfather Stevenson. Like what color hair did he have?"

She moved the cereal box aside. "Well, we only saw him a few times. He lived so far away. But I remember the oil painting he did that hung in our living room. It was a waterfall scene."

"*Mom*, that's not what I asked."

50

"Oh . . . let's see. I remember your great-grandfather didn't have much."

"Much?"

"Hair. Not when I knew him, anyway." Mom started to get up. "Come to think of it, I do remember something else."

Hubie leaned forward. "Yeah?"

"Seems that when he was younger he had red hair." She leaned over and ruffled his hair. "Probably a lot like yours," she said, smiling. Mom began rushing around the kitchen, clearing the table and rinsing the dishes. "Time to clear out, boys. I have to get to work early today."

Hubie was halfway into the living room when Mom reminded Stevie and him, "Brush your teeth! Your father and I can't afford any more dental bills."

Stevie raced him upstairs, but Hubie got to the bathroom first. And to the toothpaste. Any other time Hubie would have screwed the top back on the toothpaste tube so tight Stevie wouldn't be able to budge it. But since Stevie was already in a lousy mood, Hubie decided not to bug him anymore. They brushed in silence.

"Hubie?"

"Don't talk with your mouth full of toothpaste," he mumbled before spitting into the sink and rinsing his mouth.

Stevie was putting his toothbrush in the rack when he asked, "Are ya still mad?"

"Nah."

"Then I can jog to school with you guys?"

"Maybe."

Downstairs, Mom was putting on her coat. She reminded Stevie to take his Rocketman lunch box. He was always forgetting it. Food was one thing Hubie never ever forgot.

Before leaving, Hubie closed Fred Ferkle up in the bathroom. But first Hubie made sure there was plenty of fresh water and food. Fred rubbed his thin body against Hubie and purred, as if begging to be let out. Fred hated to be cooped up. But Mom didn't trust him anymore, not since yesterday, when he missed his litter box by two rooms. Brenda said he was senile, too old to know better. Hubie figured it had been an accident.

Stevie was waiting on the front porch steps. "Come on," Hubie called when he saw Mom backing the Chevy out of the garage. Stevie followed him to the end of the driveway, where they stood and waved their thumbs. "Give us a lift, Ma." The car stopped. Stevie slid into the backseat, Hubie got in front.

"Whatever happened to the 'I need the exercise' part?" she asked. "Aren't you and Frank jogging anymore?"

"Can't a guy sometimes ride?" Hubie answered, slamming the door shut. Drawing in his new sketch pad till after midnight had made him tired enough. Hubie wasn't about to jog to school and end up POA—Pooped On Arrival. "Besides," he added, "*you* always ride to work."

She looked at him from the corner of her eye. "My job is considerably farther away than Love School."

When Mom turned onto North Main, he saw Frank. Hubie could pick him out a mile away because he had this funny walk. Actually it was more of a bounce than a walk. Rolling down the window, he hollered. *"Hey, Frank, hustle your skinny buns over here."* Hubie felt Mom's frown bore into him.

She dropped Stevie off first, and then let Hubie and Frank off on School Street by the south entrance. They were nearing their classroom when Frank elbowed him. "Hey, look over there," whispered Frank, nodding to the left.

Marruci, leaning against a locker, had a stupid grin plastered all over his face. Then Hubie noticed who stood beside him—Shelly Hoff. A lot of guys considered her the best-looking girl in fifth grade. Of course, she didn't compare with Ms. Slomonsky.

When Marruci saw them, he called out, "Hey, this area is for fifth graders. Kindergarten is on the first floor." He laughed so hard it looked like he was going to split his Levi's.

Hubie shot right back, "Then you should be in the basement, geek," and hustled into the room.

He wasn't there long when Mrs. Bunce motioned to someone in his direction to come up front. Hubie looked over his shoulder to see whom she wanted. Since nobody seemed to be close enough, he slowly approached her. Mrs. Bunce waited in silence, drumming her fingers into the top of the desk. The flashing gold ring on her little finger caught his eye. Then he noticed what was under her hand.

"Look familiar, Hubert?" Mrs. Bunce asked, picking up the crumpled paper.

He gasped.

. . . The moving ax crunches through skin and bone. Blood gushes out, forming a crimson waterfall as Hubie's head drops to the ground. When it rolls over he sees the rest of his body still propped up on his knees.

"That takes care of ten pounds of ugly fat," says the executioner, rubbing her chubby hands together. . . .

6

How did Mrs. Bunce get hold of the picture he'd drawn of her? Hubie didn't have to wonder long. Two rows away sat Marruci, snickering back at him.

"Since you seem to have misplaced this, Hubert," began Mrs. Bunce, holding out the drawing, "I'm returning it."

He decided it wasn't a good idea to deny he'd drawn it—even the captions looked like his handwriting. Taking the picture, Hubie turned and headed for his seat. He was about to pass Marruci's desk when a boot shot out, tripping him.

"You did that on purpose," yelled Hubie.

"So what are you going to do about it . . . huh?"

Hubie felt at least ten pairs of eyes zoom in on him. Slowly, he shuffled past and slumped into his chair.

Raising his fist, Hubie shoved it hard into the side of the desk.

. . ."Boom Boom is down," the announcer shouts into the microphone. "It was Marruci's right to the head that got him." The roar of the crowd fills the steamy air.

"One," counts the referee. "Two, three, four, five—"

"What's this?" The announcer jumps to his feet and yells, "Boom Boom is struggling to get up. But will he make it in time?"

"Eight . . ."

Someone jabbed his arm. "Hey, wake up or you'll be left behind." It was Frank. Grabbing his music book, Hubie hurried out the door.

On the way home from school, Hubie told Frank that Marruci had stuck it to him once too often. "This time I'm really getting even."

"You and me both."

"The problem is *how*."

They jogged along the next few minutes in silence before Frank abruptly stopped. "I've got it! It's so simple I can't believe I didn't think of it before."

"So, I'm waiting."

"If you and me get together and ambush him," Frank said with a wide grin, "we could beat up the creep."

"Are you crazy? While he's pinning you to the ground, he'd be whipping me into Jell-O pudding."

"Whatever happened to your bodybuilding program, huh?" asked Frank.

Ignoring him, Hubie went on. "Besides, even if we did beat up the jerk, you know how my Dad feels about that."

"Yeah. Your old man has funny ideas."

Hubie gave Frank a sour look. "We've got to come up with a *good* idea."

But that wasn't so easy. Hubie thought of stuffing Marruci's clothes into an empty locker while he was taking a shower after gym. But that wouldn't work either, because Coach Vincent always checked to make sure everybody took a shower.

For the rest of the week Hubie and Frank kept coming up with new ideas. And then, just as fast, they'd scrap them. It had to be good, *really* good.

Of course, Hubie didn't spend all his time thinking about getting even with Marruci. He worked in his sketch pad too. One of his best drawings was of Fred Ferkle crouched on a limb of the old maple tree outside his bedroom window.

By Monday he still hadn't come up with an idea. After lunch, Hubie grabbed his sketch pad and lined up with the class. When they got to the art room, Ms. Slomonsky was coming out, her arms loaded down with tempera paint cans and art brushes. "I'll be right back. Stay in your assigned seats," she ordered.

Hubie dropped the pad on the table and hurried over to her. "Can I help?"

"Looks like I can use it." She smiled at him.

He noticed she had the softest brown eyes he'd ever seen. In no time Hubie found his arms encircling several paint cans. He followed her into the supply room directly across the hall. Ms. Slomonsky took the containers from him and lined them up on a shelf. "Thanks . . ." She hesitated as if she was trying to remember something.

"Hubie . . . Hubie Hartzel," he reminded her. Some impression *he* had made.

"Thanks, Hubie." And then she smiled again.

. . . Suddenly she is in his arms. "I noticed you the very first day," she says breathlessly. "I couldn't keep my eyes off you."

"I didn't know you felt the same." His head is spinning . . .

Hubie figured he must have been standing there like an idiot because she had to tell him, "We can go back now." Later in the classroom he showed her his sketch of Fred Ferkle. "I really like the way you balanced the cat and tree with the building in the background. Very nice lines here," she pointed out.

"Hey everybody," called Rob Halerman, "you should see the drawing Hubie did. Boy, is it good."

Beth Pringle, sitting across the table, leaned over. "Not half bad," she said, ogling Hubie's picture. "Actually it's pretty good."

Soon others were pushing around him, trying to get a look. Everybody talked at once and said things like "The cat looks for real" and "I didn't know you could draw."

Everybody but Marruci. "I don't think it's so great," he snorted.

Hubie ignored him.

Finally, Ms. Slomonsky told them to get back

to their seats—pronto! Then she reminded the class that she would turn on the radio the last ten minutes *if* they worked quietly the first thirty.

On the way back to the classroom most everyone agreed—Ms. Slomonsky was okay for a teacher. "She didn't turn the radio up enough," grumbled Marruci, elbowing his way over to Shelly.

Just then a forty-thousand-watt idea switched on in Hubie's head. It was so brilliant he couldn't believe his good luck.

7

Frank was mumbling about being the last person at Love School to see Hubie's drawing. Jabbing his thumb at himself, he asked, "Hey, aren't I your best friend?"

Hubie nodded. "Sure, but I—"

"Aren't best friends supposed to share everything?"

Not quite, Hubie thought. He wasn't about to tell Frank how he felt about Ms. Slomonsky. "I'll show you the drawing after I tell you my idea," said Hubie, and whispered the plan in Frank's ear. "What do you think?"

"It's the perfect scheme." Frank started grinning and rubbing his hands together like the villain in an old silent movie. "So when do we start?"

"Saturday," Hubie whispered back.

He was supposed to be at Frank's house by nine sharp to start work on Operation Harassment. That's the code name Hubie and Frank decided on. Just like in the military. But that morning Hubie had to postpone their top-secret meeting because Mom ordered Stevie and him to clean their bedroom. Naturally he protested.

"I know what," Mom said, plunking the vacuum cleaner down beside Hubie. "Pretend you've claimed enemy turf. And you boys are clearing the area of booby traps."

"Not funny, Ma. Besides, it's Stevie who makes the mess. I pick up *my* stuff."

"Then the trail of crumbs that leads directly to your bed was left by an Oreo-eating cookie monster," said Mom, crossing her arms.

Hubie grinned. "Guess he must've found your secret hiding place again."

"Humph." She spun around, walked to the doorway, and paused. "No more messes," she warned.

"I think you'd better get yourself a veggie-eating monster instead."

Mom liked to divvy out the sweets, especially to him. But he figured she was partly mad this time because now she would have to find another place to stash the goods. Before she left, Hubie asked, "When can I go over to Frank's?"

"After you've vacuumed and dusted the bedroom with Stevie, fed Fred, and cleaned out the litter box."

Fortunately, a new kitchen carpet was going to be installed any minute. Or she would have thought of more things for him to do.

It was almost ten thirty before Hubie finished his duties. As he was opening the front door to leave, Fred flew past his feet and into the house. "Oh, no you don't," Hubie said, grabbing the cat's hind legs just in time. "Mom doesn't want you in while the rug layers are working."

Looking up, he saw the reason Fred was so eager to get inside. Bounding down the street was Moose, the new neighbor's bulldog. When Moose spotted Fred, he let out a long, deep growl. Fred dug his claws into Hubie's arm.

"Scram!" Hubie hollered, throwing a stone over

Moose's head. Moose slowly turned his broad back and waddled away.

"You're safe as long as you stay on the porch," Hubie said, putting Fred down. But when Fred kept rubbing against Hubie's leg and purring, he weakened. "Okay, okay. You can come too." Since it was starting to rain, he bundled Fred under one arm and headed for his bike in the garage.

Hubie figured there were lots of advantages to being an only child. Even though Frank didn't think so. For one thing, Frank had his own bedroom. That meant he had all the privacy he wanted—something Hubie rarely got. And another thing, Frank's mother was always shoving food at him, and at Hubie, when he visited. Unlike his own mother, Mrs. Vitanza thought Hubie's weight was just right. And she was always worrying about Frank's being too skinny. Actually, Frank did look a little underfed.

When they stopped for lunch, Mrs. Vitanza had pizza waiting for them—the kind Hubie liked. Thick crust with pepperoni, Italian sausage, green peppers, onions and black olives piled high. And the mozzarella was so thick it dribbled down the sides.

Hubie nudged Frank. "Boy, what I wouldn't give to be your parents' adopted kid. Even for a week."

"Being adopted is no piece of cake. I can't do anything without them worrying. Sometimes I think they even worry about the adoption agency taking me back if I don't get the best care."

"At least you're treated special," said Hubie. "That's more than I get at home."

Before going back upstairs, Hubie picked up Frank's uneaten chocolate chip cookies. "Why didn't you want these?" Hubie asked as they trudged into the bedroom.

"Can't you think of anything besides food?" Frank made a face.

"Thinking is hard work. Besides, I need nourishment." Hubie stuffed a whole cookie into his mouth.

"Oh, *brother*."

Hubie sat on the bed and leaned against the headboard. "Why don't you read your draft first?" he said, biting into another cookie.

Frank picked up the paper he had been working

on and cleared his throat. Shaking the paper twice, he cleared his throat again.

"For Pete's sake! You're not supposed to give a sermon," Hubie mumbled. "Just read it."

One more throat clearing and Frank started to read. "Dear Ralph," he began in a voice like Miss Piggy's. "I just *adore* boys like you." Frank wriggled his hips as he sashayed across the room. "Big, strong, and handsome with a terrible . . . ahem . . . *terrific* sense of humor. And you have plenty of that!"

Hubie was laughing so hard his sides began to ache.

Frank pranced around some more, one hand on his hip. "I *must* see you after baton practice today in front of Mrs. Wiggers' room. This is our last chance to be together before I leave. Just the two of us . . . alone. But let's keep it our very own little secret. Don't mention this to anyone. Not even each other." Then he added breathlessly, "Our hearts throb—" Frank paused, looking over at Hubie. "How do you like 'throb'? Better than 'beat,' don't you think?"

"Yeah, it really grabs me."

"Ahem." Frank shifted his voice back to soprano.

"Our hearts throb as one. P.S. I can't *wait* until three thirty."

"Oh, sick. It's so disgusting it's great!"

Frank sat on the edge of the bed. "Do you think we should add a pair of red lip prints at the bottom here?"

"That's better yet," Hubie said. "When Marruci lays eyes on this he'll be panting all the way to Wiggers' room Friday."

Shelly and her family were moving to Connecticut next week. That meant Shelly and Marruci would never have a chance to get together and figure out who really wrote the notes. The timing was perfect.

. . . Marruci grasps the note to his breast. "My love calls to me," he croons, a look of ecstasy on his face as he twirls on the tips of his ballet slippers. He stops. Across the dance floor he sees his love.

"Here I come, my love, my joy." Making a wide sweep with his arms, Marruci begins running to her, his slippers barely touching the ground. The music swells as he leaps into the air. He is descending when his Listerine smile fades.

In his love's right hand is a dagger. . . .

Frank shoved Hubie off the bed. "Now it's your turn."

Picking up his draft, Hubie began to mimic Marruci's macho strut around the room. "Hey, Shelly, baby. You lucked out when I chose you to meet me in front of Old Lady Wiggers' room today after baton practice. I always had a thing for curly, short-haired blondes. Why don't you cut your hair? I think it would look less stringy. And I *do* love your smile. That two-inch gap between your front teeth is *so cute.*

"Don't miss the biggest opportunity of your life," Hubie continued. "Be sure to be at Wiggers' by three thirty sharp. But you'd better keep this to yourself. Or I'll tell everyone that you and the class geek were holding hands under the cafeteria table. Your Secret Admirer."

Frank was rolling all over the bed laughing. When he finally simmered down long enough to catch his breath, he asked, "Did they *really?*"

"Did they what?"

"You know . . . hold hands."

"How should I know?" Hubie said, shrugging. "I just put that in to make sure she meets him."

Frank remembered seeing an old portable typewriter in the attic. He found it and together the boys lugged it into the bedroom. "It works!" Frank exclaimed, punching a few keys with his forefinger.

"Barely," Hubie added as he examined the smudged letters.

For the note to Marruci, Frank used his mother's lavender notepaper with a floral design at the top. For the one to Shelly, they decided on a torn piece of paper that was slightly crumpled.

They were still typing the notes when Mrs. Vitanza called from the bottom of the staircase. "Hubie, your mother phoned. She wants you home."

Since Frank had the typewriter, he said he'd finish the notes. In the kitchen, Hubie thanked Frank's mother for lunch. Before leaving, he scooped up Fred and tucked him under his arm. Together they whizzed home on the bike, trying to outrun the raindrops.

Hubie barely got through the door and past the kitchen when Brenda belted out a scream that almost shook the green-and-white wallpaper loose from the walls. *"Mother, he's got mud all over the new kitchen carpet!"*

Hubie looked behind him at the clods of mud leading up to where he stood. He was in for it now!

8

Hubie started to backtrack.

But he didn't get far when Dad roared, "Stay put! Take your shoes off right there."

"I . . . I forgot—"

"We can't afford to replace this carpet for a long time. From now on you'll have to leave your sneakers by the back door."

Hubie couldn't decide what was worse: getting hollered at or vacuuming the carpet a zillion times. At least he wasn't the only one in trouble. Brenda was too, because she'd showed up past midnight after the homecoming dance.

All the yelling between his parents and Brenda woke Hubie up. The next thing he heard was Brenda bolting up the stairs into her bedroom and slamming the door. Long after Mom and Dad had gone to bed, he could still hear Brenda moving around. Since Brenda's room was next to his, Hubie could hear most everything.

Getting up, he knocked on her door. "Brenda?"

"Get lost!"

Opening the door a crack, he saw Brenda sitting on the edge of the bed, a cigarette dangling from her mouth. "Holy Toledo!" he blurted out.

"Didn't I tell you to get lost?" she said, between coughing and sputtering. "You tell on me, Hubie, and I'll break—"

"I won't tell a soul . . . *I swear.*"

"Shhh," Brenda whispered. "I hope for your sake Mom or Dad didn't wake up."

He held his breath as they listened. The house stayed as silent as a cemetery. "Brenda," he whispered back, "when did you start smoking?"

"None of your business," she answered, taking another puff. When she inhaled, she started coughing again.

"That stuff causes cancer. And who knows what else? I learned all about it in health class."

. . . "Hubie, I should have listened to you."
Brenda is lying on a hospital bed, her sunken eyes
look up at him. "But it's . . . too . . . late."

"No, no," he says, shaking her bony shoulders.
"You can't die yet."

Her eyes close. "Good-bye, Hubie," she whispers. . . .

"Did I ask for your opinion?" Brenda demanded,
grinding the butt into a dish. Then she picked
up the dish and tiptoed into the hall.

Hubie knew what she had done with the evidence when he heard the toilet flush. When
Brenda returned, she was holding her forehead
and groaning.

"Can I do something for you?" asked Hubie.
"Like get you a drink of water?" Brenda didn't
look too well.

"No thanks . . . Hubie?"

"Yeah?"

"Sorry I yelled at you."

"Sure. Actually, your zits aren't all that bad."
Hubie paused by the door. "You're not going to
smoke anymore, are you?"

Brenda didn't answer. Instead, cupping her
hands over her mouth, she shoved past him and
raced for the bathroom.

Having carpet in the kitchen was a real pain. Now every time Hubie put one foot inside, he'd hear: "Did you leave your shoes by the back door?" At supper last night it was even worse.

"Eat over your plate," Dad ordered just because one measly crumb fell to the floor. But after what happened this morning, he figured Dad wouldn't bug him about it anymore.

It all started around nine thirty last night, when Hubie hit on a real bonanza. He found where Mom stashed this week's supply of cookies. She was always changing the hiding places.

The reason Hubie lucked out was because of the hole he made in his math paper when he erased a mistake. He went straight for the kitchen drawer where Mom kept the tape. Hubie was reaching inside when he noticed something shoved way in the back of the drawer. Since it barely fit the small space, he had to tug it forward.

"Holy Toledo," he muttered when he saw that it was an unopened package of Double-Stuf Oreo cookies.

Later that night, Hubie pretended to sniff the air. "Funny thing," he said. "But something smells an awful lot like . . ." He cocked his head to one side as though trying to guess the source of the mysterious smell. Then, grinning, Hubie added, "Just like Double-Stuf Oreo cookies."

Mom glanced sidelong at him. "Funny thing," she repeated.

"Sure wish I had an Oreo right now."

"Someone mention Oreo cookies?" Dad looked up, the sports section of the *Post-Journal* dangling from his hand.

It took both Dad and Hubie hungrily staring at the drawer that Mom was guarding like a sentry before she finally relented. "Oh, all right." She stepped aside. They moved in like vultures after the kill. "But make sure there are enough left over for Brenda and Stevie."

Dad poured milk while Hubie dealt out the Oreos. Five for Dad, five for him. Then he put the rest in the cookie jar. Hubie could never figure out why they even owned a cookie jar. It was hardly ever used.

After eating his five, Hubie pleaded, "Just one more to go with the rest of my milk?"

Dad shook his head. "Maybe I should padlock the cookie jar." He started laughing like he had said something really funny. Some dumb joke. Then because it was almost ten o'clock he sent Hubie to bed.

The next morning, Hubie was pouring milk into his bowl of Monster Chocula, and Dad came into the kitchen. Hubie figured that Dad must have eyes like a hawk because he was always noticing dirt or crumbs on the new carpet. That morning, his hawk eyes zoomed in on something. "What's that!" he demanded.

Everyone looked down past the cookie jar and the line of canisters to the floor where Dad pointed. There was a dark blob on the carpet.

"Fred had another accident," Stevie hollered.

"No he didn't, stupid! Fred isn't allowed in the kitchen anymore," Hubie said.

Dad picked up whatever it was with a paper towel, tossed it into the garbage and sat down.

"What was it?" Hubie asked.

Dad chewed a mouthful of toast while everyone waited. Finally he mumbled, "Piece of cookie."

Hubie wondered why Dad didn't ask *who* had pilfered the cookie jar. Now Hubie felt Mom looking at him suspiciously. "Hold it," Hubie said, bristling. "I went to bed right after the snack."

"Snack? What snack?" Stevie shouted. "I get sent to bed early and you guys get to stay up and . . . and *eat cookies*!"

"Shut up," Hubie said under his breath. He wanted to know exactly who had snitched the Oreos and left behind the evidence. This was getting very interesting. Hubie figured it couldn't have been Brenda. She was still into health foods—no sweets. And Stevie didn't even know about the Oreos. He looked at Mom.

"Not me," she said, shrugging.

Three heads swung toward Dad.

Stevie burst out in a singsong: "Daddy is the cookie monster; Daddy is the cookie monster." Then he laughed like crazy.

"Hey, Dad," called Hubie. "Looks like *I'll* have to padlock the cookie jar."

"I'm late for work," said Dad, grinning sheepishly as he got up. "Bye-bye, my little chick-adees."

Frank was waiting for him at their usual place. "What took you so darn long?" he snapped, flinging his arms in the air.

Hubie didn't answer. He was still chuckling

to himself. "You won't *believe* what happened this morning. My dad got caught—"

"Will you shut up for a second?" said Frank with a worried look on his face. "We've got a problem."

9

Frank had hidden the notes in the drawer where he kept his clean underwear, and if he hadn't used up the last pair, Mrs. Vitanza would never have discovered the notes.

"How'd I know she was going to do a wash Sunday night?" said Frank, shrugging. "I told her it was a creative writing assignment. I don't think she believed me though. She ripped them up before making me haul the typewriter back to the attic."

"You've still got the original notes we wrote, don't you?" Hubie was trying to remember exactly what they had written.

Frank drew two crumpled papers out of his back pocket and handed them to Hubie. "At least she didn't wash my jeans."

"Looks like we'll just have to write them ourselves."

"Yeah, sure. It wouldn't take much of a brain to figure out who wrote them. Even a moron like Marruci can do that."

"Not if the notes are forged," Hubie said.

"I don't know any good forgers."

Winking at him, Hubie answered, "I do . . . you and me."

Of course that meant they'd have to get samples of Marruci's and Shelly's handwriting. Marruci wouldn't be a problem. Since the inside of his desk resembled a battlefield, Hubie figured Marruci would never miss one lousy paper.

But Shelly was a different matter. She was so organized, the inside of her desk looked unused. Hubie was positive she'd know if something was missing. And retrieving one of her papers from the wastepaper basket was definitely out. Shelly never threw anything away. She was so neat it made him want to puke.

It was lunchtime before Hubie finally came up

with an idea. He mentioned it to Frank as they sat at the far end of the cafeteria table. "So how are you going to do it?" Frank asked, unwrapping his lunch. He bit into a pickle-and-cheese sandwich. Frank had weird taste buds.

"You mean, how are *you* going to do it?"

"Me!" Frank almost choked on a pickle.

"Since you sit behind Shelly, it would be a lot easier if you did it."

"Sure, easy for you to say."

Hubie was about to say something when he noticed Beth Pringle get up from a nearby table. She sashayed over to them and sat on the bench beside Frank. "You guys look like you're having a secret meeting." She flashed her best smile at Frank. "Is that so, Frankie?"

Frank's eyes turned into saucers as he gulped down his food. "Oh, ah, we were just talking about—"

"Mrs. Harrison having twins," Hubie blurted out.

"That's been around for so long nobody even talks about it anymore." Beth turned her attentions to Frank, sliding closer to him until their shoulders touched. "I'll just bet you have something more interesting to tell. Right, Frankie?" She gave him her Miss Beauty Contestant smile and waited.

Frank melted before their very eyes. "Ahhh, well . . ."

In order to save Frank's skin, Hubie threw in a clincher. "Mrs. Harrison is expecting again in September."

Beth's Grand Canyon mouth formed a perfect O as she covered it with her hand. "Oh, my. So soon?"

"Do you mean," Hubie said, raising his voice, "you're the *last* to know?"

"Of course not," insisted Beth, abruptly getting up. "I knew that last week." Whirling, she went over to the next table and plopped down on the bench.

"She called me Frankie," Frank kept muttering to himself. He had a faraway look on his face.

. . . "Frank, you've got to get hold of yourself." Hubie tries shaking Frank, but that doesn't pull him out of his stupor.

"She called me Frankie."

"You can't go on like this any longer. It's already ruined forty-nine years of your life. Beth married somebody else forty years ago. Face it, Frank. She's a great-grandmother. And she's fat and ugly."

84

"She called me Frankie." Frank's smile is etched like the creases in his face. "She called me Frankie. . . ."

"Earth calling Frankie. Earth calling Frankie. Are you there, Frankie?"

"Shut up."

"Okay, okay. But let's get back to our plans." Hubie looked around to make sure nobody was listening. "Look, all you have to do is tell Shelly you don't understand today's English assignment." One thing about girls like Shelly and Beth, they liked to show off how smart they were. "Have a paper ready and tell her to write on that."

Frank opened a wedge-shaped plastic container. Inside was a piece of homemade pie. Hubie's mouth started to water when the smell of cinnamon and apples drifted past his nose.

"I still don't see why you can't do it," Frank said, sinking the plastic fork into the flaky crust.

"I told you *why*. . . . Boy, that pie sure looks awfully good." Hubie stared at his orange. "I'll trade you my newest Stuntman comic book for—"

"Not on your life." Then Frank took a big bite.

Hubie stayed late to finish his math assignment. That meant he had to wait until after supper to work on Operation Harassment.

Frank came over to Hubie's house with the sample.

"Great," Hubie said when Frank handed it to him. "See . . . that wasn't so bad."

Frank rolled his eyes. "The heck it wasn't. When I told Shelly that I didn't understand the assignment, she went on and on about prepositional phrases. I thought she'd *never* shut up!"

Moving Fred Ferkle aside, Hubie plunked down on his bed and examined Shelly's handwriting. First he traced over her rounded letters. Then he tried to write like Shelly on another paper.

Frank scrunched up his face. "That doesn't look at all like her writing," he said, and tried it himself.

"Not bad," said Hubie, looking over Frank's shoulder. "But that loop isn't quite—"

Frank threw down the pencil and started for the door.

"What's bugging you?"

"I got Shelly's writing. Now *you* forge the note!"

"Hey, wait. It really looks good. . . . Ah, come on, Frank." Since Marruci's handwriting looked like chicken tracks, Hubie decided he could fake Marruci's note with no problem. As for Shelly's, he wasn't so sure.

Hubie had finally talked Frank into helping him when Stevie barged into the bedroom and jumped onto his bed. He sat there staring at them.

"Whatcha doing?" asked Stevie.

"Don't you have something better to do?"

"Nope."

"We can finish this tomorrow," said Frank, getting up. "Besides, I have to be home before eight."

Except for Stevie goofing up that night's work, Operation Harassment was going along just great—until the next morning.

That's when things started to go haywire.

10

That morning, Hubie found out what was really bugging Frank.

They were racing into the classroom, two steps ahead of the tardy bell, when Frank bumped into Beth Pringle.

"Gee, I'm sorry," Frank said, grinning at her. "Can I help you with that?"

Taking a step back and adjusting her tower of books, Beth pushed past Frank. Her nose scraped the ceiling.

That's when Frank turned on Hubie. "It's all

your fault!" he whispered gruffly. "It had to be *my* job to get Shelly's handwriting. Now Beth thinks just because I asked Shelly about that dumb English assignment I like her instead."

"I don't understand what you even see in that oversized potato chip."

Frank gave Hubie a look that cooled his words. "Look who's talking," he said before charging over to his desk.

They didn't speak to each other the rest of the day. Hubie decided he wasn't going to be the first to say something.

That night after Stevie had fallen asleep Hubie lifted up the edge of his mattress and pulled out his sketch pad and Operation Harassment notes. Along with the notes there was a drawing he didn't want certain people to see—especially Stevie, the blabbermouth. It would be okay if anyone saw the covered bridge he'd drawn and the drawings of funny faces of people he knew. But *not* the portrait he'd drawn of Ms. Slomonsky. Tomorrow he was planning to give it to her.

Hubie tried to finish the note to Marruci. That wasn't so easy. No matter how hard he tried, it just didn't look like Shelly's handwriting. Hubie finally gave up. He was too tired, he decided, stuffing his things back under the mattress. Yawning, he fell asleep.

The next day Frank still ignored him. Once during English class Hubie did his best to be friendly. When Frank needed more notepaper, Hubie tried to give him some of his. Instead, Frank took Rob's.

Hubie was glad when the three-o'clock bell finally rang. He went straight to the art room. It was locked. He was trying to decide what to do next when he saw Ms. Slomonsky and Coach Vincent turn the far corner. They walked so close together their bodies touched. He was doing all the talking and she was laughing. Hubie didn't like the way Coach looked at her.

He started to walk in the opposite direction, hoping they wouldn't notice him.

"Hubie," Ms. Slomonsky called. "Were you waiting for me?"

Turning, he stammered, "Ah . . . I, ah . . . brought my sketches."

"I'd like to see them." Then quietly she said something to Coach and he left.

Hubie watched Ms. Slomonsky, her hair swinging loosely down her back, as she unlocked the door. "Okay," she said, flinging the keys on her desk. "Let's see what you have."

Hubie opened the pad to the covered bridge drawing he had copied from a magazine, and handed it to her. His heart started to thud so loudly he was sure she could hear it too. He held his breath, hoping that would stop it.

"I like it," she said.

Whooosh. Letting his breath go, Hubie started to feel light-headed.

She flipped through the pad, stopping at the funny faces. Her soft, airy laughter sounded like the wind chimes his mother hung each summer on the front porch. "You certainly have a knack for drawing caricatures."

Frank's face looked like the upper half of a toothpick with elephant ears attached. And Mrs. Bunce looked like she could saw steel with her nose. Even her accordion chin was more sharp than rounded.

"Didn't you draw me?" Ms. Slomonsky asked. Her brown eyes pierced his.

Turning to the back of the pad, Hubie pulled out the portrait. "It's for you . . . to keep."

"How thoughtful of you. I can see that you put a lot of effort into this."

   . . . Lana takes his hands into hers. "Oh, Hubert, you are so talented. But it's your thoughtfulness I most admire about you."

   "And I admire you too, Lana. Everything about you. Everything . . ."

"Ready, Lana?" Coach stood in the doorway, his tan overcoat on.

"In a minute, Brad." Turning to Hubie, she said, "I'll treasure this."

He wasn't sure what to say next, so he grabbed his pad and started to back out of the room. When he got to the door, Hubie stumbled over his feet. His face got hot all over as he caught himself. Then he hightailed it out of the room so fast he didn't catch what she was telling him. But he wasn't about to go back and chance doing something even more stupid.

On the way home his mind spun with thoughts of Ms. Slomonsky. It was more fun to think about her than Operation Harassment. But he still hadn't decided what to do about the note. Hubie knew he'd better come up with something quick. Friday was Shelly's last day. And his only big chance to get back at Marruci.

Who could he get to forge Shelly's note? It had to be somebody with good handwriting. And somebody he could trust . . .

"Holy Toledo." Hubie snapped his fingers. "Why didn't I think of it sooner?"

11

Hubie found Brenda sprawled out on the couch in the family room watching the tail end of *As the Stomach Turns*, a better title, he decided, than the real one. "I've got to talk with you, Bren."

"Shhh. This is the good part," she whispered.

Her eyes were riveted to the TV screen. That's when Hubie decided to find out what was so great about this dumb soap. Funny he hadn't noticed before, probably because he never cared to watch, but this actress looked a lot like Ms. Slomonsky. Tears streamed down her face as the picture faded into a commercial.

When Hubie looked back at the couch, Brenda was gone. "Hey," he hollered, racing upstairs after her. "Wait up for—"

Brenda slammed the door in his face.

"I've got to talk with you. It's really important!" Pausing, Hubie waited to see if Brenda would open up. She didn't. "It . . . it's practically life or death." Of course, he didn't say whose life or whose death. But she finally did open the door.

Draped over her arm was the costume she'd be wearing in the school play the following weekend—a nun's habit. "That serious, huh?"

He nodded.

She moved aside. Hubie sat on the pink-and-white calico bedspread, careful not to mess it up. Brenda was picky about things like that. Everything in her room was either ruffled, quilted or both.

He waited while Brenda pulled the costume over her jeans. Taking the headpiece out of a large box, she stood before a full-length mirror and put it on.

"You look like a real nun," Hubie said, not quite believing the change from his flaky sister to this sweetly smiling stranger.

"You really think so?" Brenda adjusted the head-piece. "I just hope I don't forget my lines. Or, worse yet, what if I'm off-key for my big solo?"

"That won't happen."

"Easy for you to say," she answered. "But when my tongue gets tangled up in my braces—"

"With your talent, it'll be a snap." He wanted her in a good mood.

Brenda eyed him suspiciously. "Okay," she finally said as she pulled off the costume. "So what's this 'life or death' problem of yours that can't wait?"

While she put the costume back in the boxes, he told her everything that led up to Operation Harassment. Well, not quite everything. Just the important stuff. Then, since he had memorized the letters, Hubie recited them to her.

"I can't believe my little brother actually thought this scheme up."

Hubie didn't like the part about "little." Stevie should be considered little, not him. But he decided not to push his luck. So he kept his mouth shut about that. Instead, he told her he needed help forging Shelly's letter. "I can't do it without you," he said. "You *will* help . . . won't you?"

97

Brenda thought it over a moment. "I don't know . . ."

"Pleeese?" Hubie was prepared to get down on his knees and beg if he had to.

"I don't know if I can. Besides, I'll need something to copy from, and you don't—"

"Hold on," he said, jumping up. Before Brenda could draw another breath, Hubie had dashed to his room and back. Handing the sample to her, he said, "Thanks, Bren."

Reluctantly she took the paper. "I just hope I'm not making a big mistake."

Around midnight Hubie's nose started a slow drip that turned into Niagara Falls by the next morning. Any other day he would have complained and gotten to stay home. It was just his rotten luck to get a head cold on D day.

Since it was starting to drizzle, Mom made him wear his yellow slicker. He could understand why Stevie had to wear one. But him? He must have told her at least a zillion times that nobody, absolutely *nobody* in fifth grade wore a slicker. She didn't listen this time either. Too bad it wasn't Mom's turn to drive to work or she would have driven Stevie and him to school.

He made it three houses down from his without anyone noticing. Taking off the wet coat and stuffing it into his duffel bag, Hubie noticed Frank walking with Rob Halerman. He kicked a stone and watched it fly through the air before bumping into a tree. He sure wasn't going to let that bother him, he decided. Anyway, he had more important matters to think about. Like the last details to Operation Harassment.

Hubie decided to wait until lunch to slip the notes into Marruci's and Shelly's lockers. All morning he kept checking his back pocket to make sure the notes were still there. He wore his Steelers pullover so nobody could see them sticking up. But he had to be careful because whenever he sat they would pop out from under his jersey. His other pockets were stuffed with tissues.

In the cafeteria, about fifteen minutes into lunch, Hubie started to cough hard on purpose. He wanted the monitor's attention. Instead he got Beth's. Without warning, she walked up to him and walloped him on the back so hard he practically had whiplash. This not only cleared his stuffed-up nose, it also shook his teeth so they crash-landed on his tongue. Hubie was in agony when the monitor finally noticed him.

"Water!" he blurted out. *"I need water!"* Then, without waiting for permission, he raced for the water fountain just outside the cafeteria. As the cool water splashed against his throbbing tongue, Hubie looked through the open doorway. Beth, the busybody, was charging across the cafeteria.

When he looked up again he saw Beth poised over him like a five-star general. Her hands, curled into fists, were shoved against her hips.

Hubie stood at attention.

"So, Mrs. Harrison is expecting." Her red leather loafer hit the linoleum. *Tap, tap.* "In September, huh?" *Tap, tap, tap.*

Hubie looked around. She had him cornered.

"That's not exactly what I said."

Beth leaned forward, closing the gap between them as she raised her voice. *"I know perfectly well what you said."*

She was going to ruin everything. If the monitor discovered them she would send them back to the cafeteria for sure. Then he might as well kiss Operation Harassment good-bye. "What I said was . . ." began Hubie. He paused to make sure the words sunk in. "What I *really* said was, Mrs. Harrison is expecting to be back in September."

Beth's stare bored into him like a diamond-studded drill. But instead of the cavalry charge Hubie expected, she whirled and marched into the nearby girls' bathroom.

"Phew." Hubie quickly looked around. Good, he was safe, he decided as he bounded upstairs to the second floor. Fifth-grade lockers were down the hall, to the right. Hubie slowed down when he saw the custodian pushing a wide mop toward him. Staring at the tile floor, he tried to blend in with the mint-green walls. After the custodian turned the corner, Hubie hurried over to Marruci's locker and looked down the long hallway. It was deserted. Yanking the notes out of his back pocket, he separated Marruci's. As he was shoving it through the air vent, he noticed something to the left flash by. When Hubie turned to look, whoever it was had disappeared.

Eight lockers down he did the same with Shelly's note. Only this time he made sure nobody was around to see.

When Hubie returned to the cafeteria, Frank's and his eyes locked for a second. Since Frank knew

today was D day, he probably knew what Hubie had been up to. Even though they weren't on what you'd call "friendly terms," Hubie decided he could still count on Frank to keep his mouth shut.

A couple of minutes later Beth swept into the cafeteria. She smiled at Hubie as she passed his table. He sure couldn't figure girls out. Just five minutes ago she had been ready to string him up by his tongue.

Marruci found his note right after lunch. The rest of the day he kept making eyes at Shelly, who tried to ignore him. Ignoring Marruci was a little like ignoring a stampeding buffalo.

After class Shelly went straight to her locker to clean it out. Beth and Tammy stood nearby making a big scene over how much they'd miss Shelly. Then Beth started talking about the going-away party they'd planned to have after school during baton practice.

Hubie took his time putting the books back into his locker. What was taking her so long? Finally, Shelly picked up the note from the floor of her locker. He saw sparks fly when she read the good parts.

Grinning, Hubie slammed the locker door shut. Revenge was near.

He had planned to spend the next twenty minutes with Ms. Slomonsky, but Mrs. Bunce made him stay to finish his math. Sometimes she'd let Pete Walker finish his at home. Then why not him? But Hubie knew her standard answer to that question: "Pete needs the extra time. You're perfectly capable of getting it done in class." Nuts. She just liked Pete better than him.

He whizzed through it so fast he was done in ten minutes. Mrs. Bunce checked his paper to make sure he hadn't fudged the answers. "Didn't miss one," she said, adding his work to the foot-high stack of papers. "Suppose you could do that more often during class?"

Hubie shuffled his feet. "I guess so."

"Hubert Hartzel, if you would just take the time to put more effort into your schoolwork you could—"

"Mrs. Bunce," a voice from the PA boomed out. "Can you come to the office for a call? Mrs. Seekings is on the line." Hubie hurried out the door right behind Mrs. Bunce.

104

He found Ms. Slomonsky taping up paintings in the hall outside the classroom. "Need some help?" he asked, watching as she stood on the fourth rung of the stepladder.

She glanced over her shoulder. "Hi, Hubie. I'm glad you're here. Can you tell me if that's straight?"

Stepping back, he looked up at the picture she held. "A little more up on the left . . . Stop!"

On the opposite wall Hubie noticed two of his pen-and-ink drawings. Mrs. Harrison had never put up any of his stuff. But then in her class everybody had been forced to make dumb things like wall hangings and collages—yuck! She never let them have a choice like Ms. Slomonsky did.

"Will you hand me that painting over there?"

He picked it up and handed it to her.

"Thanks . . . I just hope I'm ready for the Art Festival next Thursday. That reminds me. Have you thought over what I asked you the other day?"

"Huh? Ah, sort of." Hubie tried hard to remember what she was talking about, but nothing stood out. Nothing important, that is. Then he remembered her saying something to him yesterday as he was leaving. He'd been too busy tripping over his own feet. What could he say next? he wondered. His thoughts spun as he looked at the wisps of hair framing her face.

She started to climb down.

. . . Her shoe catches the bottom rung. As she starts to fall, Hubie rushes over. Suddenly his arms are encircling her and they gaze deeply into each other's eyes.

"Where have you been all my life?" she whispers.

"Waiting for you, Lana."

Her ruby lips draw closer to his. . . .

"The Art Festival will open in the auditorium with a short introduction. You'll only need to say a few words. You know, your personal feelings about the art program."

"Few words?"

"Two other students will also speak. Jonathan Wheeler for the music program and Becky Zitler for creative writing." Looking at Hubie, Ms. Slomonsky added, "I thought of you first."

Nobody *ever* thought of him first. When it came to choosing teams for softball, he was always one of the last picked. Even last year when his class put on a variety show, Mrs. Hamerstrom put him and all the other freaks in the sideshow. He was the sword swallower. Big deal. The rest of the kids got to do the good stuff.

"Few words?" Hubie repeated weakly. *Him,* speak in front of a bunch of people? "Gee, I . . . I couldn't." Looking up at her, he added, "Jon and Becky are good. Really good. I mean, they're always on the honor roll."

"And you are one of my best art students. Now . . . if you want, I'll help you compose it."

Hubie shook his head. "I really can't. I mean, I'm glad you thought of me, but I—"

"You can do it, Hubie. I want you to know that you're very special."

Special? *Him?* This was Hubie Hartzel, the overweight clod, she was talking about. Looking up into her soft, brown eyes, Hubie found himself slowly melting into his sneakers.

Before stopping to think, he blurted out, "I'll do it." That was bad enough. He couldn't believe his ears when he heard himself say, "You're the prettiest teacher here." Instead of waiting to hear what his mouth would come up with next, Hubie started backing down the hallway. "I've got to go. See ya, Ms. Slomonsky." Whirling, he took off.

As he hurried to Old Lady Wiggers' room, Hubie checked his watch. Three twenty-six. He had planned to get to his hiding place before Marruci and Shelly showed up.

He hoped he wasn't too late.

12

Nobody was around as Hubie slid into the darkened alcove beside the stairwell. While he waited, he kept thinking of Ms. Slomonsky's words and wondering what they meant. Maybe she really *did* like him. Maybe even better than she liked Coach.

Then Hubie remembered his promise. What if he said or did something stupid in front of everybody? Especially Ms. Slomonsky. The last thing he wanted to do was disappoint her.

The sound of a closing door caught his attention. Carefully, he looked around the alcove. Mrs. Wiggers was locking her door. Across from her, bent over the water fountain, was Marruci. When she left, Marruci started pacing back and forth in front of her room and checking his watch. He kept doing that for the next ten minutes.

What if Shelly didn't show up? Or, worse yet, what if she figured out it was a hoax and told Marruci? Then together they'd find out who set them up. What if . . .

That's when Hubie spotted Shelly at the far end of the hall. Marruci was leaning over the water fountain again getting another sip of water as she approached. She was swinging her baton like a cop swinging a nightstick. She stopped in front of Marruci. And waited.

Hubie felt a terrible urge to sneeze. "Ah . . . Ah . . ." Grabbing his nostrils, he pinched them together hard and swallowed. When the muffled explosion passed, he looked around the alcove again. Good, they hadn't heard him.

Marruci was now facing Shelly and grinning from ear to ear. "Hey, Shelly, baby," he began. "This is the last time we'll be alone together. Let's say we make the most of it. How 'bout a kiss?" He closed his eyes and puckered up his lips.

Instead of offering her lips, Shelly raised her baton and lowered it—not too gently, either—on his head.

"*Ouch!* That hurts." Backing away, Marruci held up his hands for protection.

"It's meant to, you jerk." Then, shaking her baton at him, she continued, "If I hear about you telling mean, spiteful things about me when I'm gone, I'll have you arrested for slander."

Marruci looked dazed. "I . . . I don't understand."

"Humph!" said Shelly, as she pushed past him.

Since there wasn't time to move away, Hubie flattened himself against the wall and prayed she wouldn't notice him. Shelly looked straight ahead as she marched down the stairs.

Marruci's head now hung so low he could have eyeballed his belly button. Before shuffling off in the opposite direction, he mumbled something about girls being a pain in the butt.

This *had* to be his lucky day, Hubie decided. Not only had he finally gotten revenge, but Ms. Slomonsky had told him he was special. *Very* special, in fact. That could mean only one thing: She felt the same for him as he did for her.

If only his head didn't feel like somebody was taking a sledgehammer to it, he could have enjoyed his triumph better. "Crummy cold," Hubie muttered, taking out his last clean tissue.

Hubie figured the peanut-butter-and-jelly sandwich he made when he got home from school would help. But after one tiny bite he just sat at the kitchen table and stared at the rest of it.

Something is definitely wrong, he decided, putting his hand on his forehead. How was he supposed to know if he was sick without a thermometer? Stevie had busted it last time he got sick. The idiot put it in hot water to "kill all the sick germs."

Stevie. That's it, Hubie decided, as he went into the living room. Stevie was on the floor playing with eight of his eighty-seven Matchbox cars.

Bending down, Hubie clamped one hand on Stevie's forehead and one on his.

Stevie jerked away.

"Let me check your forehead."

"What for?"

"I want to see if I have a fever."

Stevie looked up. "You don't look sick." Then

he went back to making zooming and crashing noises as he moved the cars around a pretend race-track.

"That's what *you* think. Come on, let me check."

"Okay."

Hubie had started to put his hand on Stevie's forehead when Stevie jerked away again.

"But only if you pay me a quarter."

"*What?* Are you crazy? You're the one who broke the thermometer in the first place." Hubie got him down to a dime, and Stevie consented.

He was comparing foreheads when Stevie burst out, "I smell peanut butter. You've been eating peanut butter."

"No I haven't."

"Yes, you have!" he screamed. "And it's on your hand."

"Keep it down," hollered Brenda from the living room. "Janet and I can't get anything done with all that racket."

"If you shut up and forget the dime," Hubie began in a quieter voice, "I'll make you a sandwich." After Hubie decided his forehead was a little warmer than Stevie's, he made a pb-and-j sandwich the way Stevie liked it—with strawberry jam so thick it oozed out the sides.

Then Hubie went straight to the couch. Mom found him there when she got home. "This isn't the Hubie Hartzel I know," she said. "Are you sick?"

"I think I have a fever."

She clamped her hand over his forehead, holding it there a while. "You have a slight fever."

"I'm not even hungry—not one bit."

"Now that *is* unusual." She started to grin. "You mean to tell me the refrigerator and cupboards are still intact from this morning?"

"It's no joke."

"Are you having any other problems? Like loose bowels?"

"Shhh." Hubie glanced toward the next room, where Brenda and her girlfriend were. "Geez, Ma. Do you have to say it so loud?" he whispered.

"Sorry," she whispered back. "But are you?"

"No."

One thing about getting sick, Hubie didn't have to go to the school musical that night. Mom stood by the door with an uncertain look on her face. "Maybe I should stay."

"Brenda would be disappointed."

"But suppose your illness took a sudden turn for the—"

Just then a honk sounded from the driveway. Dad and Stevie were already in the car.

"Go, Ma," Hubie said. "I'll be okay."

Her last words were "Remember to let Fred in before seven." That was the time Moose took his owner for a walk.

Hubie was nodding when he heard what sounded like thunder rolling down the stairs. "I'll die if I'm late for the performance," screeched Brenda as she dashed for the door.

"Good luck, Bren." Hubie flashed her a V sign.

After everybody had cleared out, Hubie took a nap. Barking and a loud yowl from outside awoke him. Rubbing his eyes, he sat up and looked at the wall clock. Seven twenty-three. "Oh, no." He'd forgotten to let Fred in. Hubie ran to the back door.

Outside he found Moose, up on his hind legs, dancing around the large maple tree behind the house. He was barking at Fred, who clung to the highest branch. Mr. Orvin finally caught up with Moose and, grabbing his rhinestone collar, hauled him away.

When Moose was gone, Hubie called, "Okay, chickenhead, come on down." But Fred didn't move a muscle. "You're even a bigger chickenhead than I thought." Hubie noticed Fred's eyes flash in the dim light—like he was saying "Look who's talking."

"Get your buns down from there *now*!" Fred still wouldn't budge. And all that yelling wasn't doing Hubie one bit of good. Even though perspiration was gathering on his back and face, Hubie shivered. "If you can get yourself up that tree," he called to Fred, "then you can darn well get yourself down." Back inside, Hubie stumbled over to the couch and lay down. Every bone in his body now ached.

. . . He hears his name called, but it sounds hollow and far away. Hubie looks up. Mr. Bottomly, the principal, is standing onstage. He is motioning for him. Lana, poised near the steps, is nodding and smiling at Hubie.

Slowly he pulls himself out of his seat. As he stands, thousands of eyes zoom in on him. Hubie tries to move, but his shoes feel like weights with magnets attached to the soles. Sweat pours off his body and lands in red pools. Finally, he makes it to the top step. Just as Lana reaches out, he slips and tumbles down the stairs.

Looking up, he sees Lana's face twisted in a look of horror. . . .

117

13

"Hubie?"

". . . *Lana* . . ."

"Hubie, wake up."

Opening his eyes, Hubie saw Mom leaning over him. He was still groggy as she shoved a thermometer into his mouth.

"That must've been some dream you were having." Dad stood in the doorway, grinning at him. "Who's Lana?"

Hubie pretended he didn't hear.

Stevie ran into the living room. He looked under the chairs and then the couch.

"What *are* you doing?" asked Mom.

"Looking for Fred. He's not in the bathroom and he's not upstairs. So I figure he's gotta be somewhere down here."

"Holy Toledo," Hubie mumbled. He pulled the thermometer out of his mouth and handed it to Mom. "Fred's stuck up that big maple tree in our yard."

"A hundred three point six," said Mom, shaking the thermometer. "I thought you looked awfully warm." Then she sent him straight to bed while Dad went to the garage to get the ladder.

The next morning Hubie awoke with a thirst that would rival Godzilla's. But the orange juice Mom brought tasted so awful it made him gag. He spent all day in bed dreaming about the way Ms. Slomonsky had looked at him when she told him he was *very* special.

Hubie figured he didn't have to worry about next Thursday. He was so sick he wouldn't be back before then. But Tuesday night his high fever took a nosedive. Mom found out when she came up to check his temperature.

"One hundred even," she said.

"Are you sure?" Hubie took the thermometer and read it himself. "Well, it'll probably go up again tomorrow." He lay back on the bed and waited for her to leave. But she just stood there, like she had something on her mind. "Where's ol' Fred Ferkle?" Hubie asked. "He hasn't even been up to visit me since . . ." Hubie's words trailed off when he noticed a funny look on Mom's face. This was one look he'd never seen before.

"That's what I want to talk with you about. Remember the other night when your father went out to get Fred?"

"Oh, no. He isn't . . ." Hubie couldn't say the word. If he did, then it would be true for sure.

"We didn't want to tell you until you were feeling better. I'm really sorry."

Hubie shook his head. "Not Fred." Tears started to well up in his eyes. "He *can't* be."

"I know this probably won't comfort you now, but Fred lived a very long life. And for all those years he had a good home."

She was right; her words didn't help. If only he had remembered to let Fred in when he was supposed to.

. . . "You left me out there with that monster." Fred Ferkle looks over the edge of a cloud. An orange fluorescent glow encircles him. "I escaped from his clutches. But all that running and climbing did this old heart no good." Pointing his paw directly at Hubie, Fred adds, "Then *you*, chickenhead, left me out there to die."

"But I was sick." The cloud starts to get smaller as it moves higher. "Wait, Fred. I didn't mean to . . ."

"I don't want you to blame yourself, Hubie. Fred was almost seventeen years old. It was only a matter of time."

How did she read his mind? he wondered.

By Wednesday morning his temperature was down to 98.9. Mom called it normal. Just as he was trying to convince her that 98.6 was normal, not 98.9, the phone rang. Mom answered.

It was Ms. Slomonsky. Mom told her that she could definitely count on Hubie being at school the next day. Mom wore a big smile as she put the phone back on the hook. "Hubie," she said, turning toward him. "Why didn't you tell me about this honor of yours?"

"I really don't think I should go back till at least Friday, Mom." Hubie hacked three good ones before adding, "What if I should get pneumonia?"

"You'll be just fine. I know you will."

So what did she do next? She called Grandma and Grandpa Hartzel and invited them to come too.

If he didn't go through with it now he'd have the whole family disappointed in him—let alone Ms. Slomonsky. Hubie tried to decide what was worse—disappoint everybody or make a fool of himself. Since the possibility of disappointing everybody was a sure thing and the other wasn't, he decided to go through with it. Besides, *he* was the one Ms. Slomonsky chose. And if she figured he could do it, then maybe he could.

By bedtime Hubie was even starting to look forward to school the next day. Hadn't Ms. Slomonsky said she would help him? Besides, he'd do anything to be with her.

He was getting ready for bed when the phone rang. "Hubie," called Brenda from the hallway. "It's for you."

"Who is it?" he asked, taking the receiver. He hoped it was Frank.

She shrugged.

"Hello?"

"I'm gonna get you, nerd," a raspy voice

screamed into his ear. "And when I do, your eyeballs will be spinning for a week." Then he heard a loud clank and silence.

Hubie felt as if someone had just punched him in the stomach. How had Marruci found out? Only two other people knew about the plan, he thought as he headed straight for the first suspect. He found Brenda propped up on her bed reading a paperback and chomping on a carrot.

Waving his fist at her, Hubie snarled, "How many people did you tell?"

"Tell what?"

"About *me* setting Marruci up!"

"Hey, I'm not a blabbermouth. Sometimes you *are* a big pain. But I'd never do a mean thing like that to my own brother."

That left only one other suspect.

14

Thursday morning Hubie left for school a half hour early. He needed the extra time so he could see Ms. Slomonsky and they could figure out what he would say that afternoon.

The art room was locked. As he turned away, Hubie thought he heard a noise coming from the supply room. Since the door was ajar, he opened it and looked inside.

At first he didn't see anyone. Then he noticed two people standing in the shadows. Coach Vincent had his arms around Ms. Slomonsky's waist, and her arms encircled his neck. They were in a clinch so tight that a rubber band wound around them ten times couldn't get them any closer. And they were kissing. It wasn't the kind of kiss he gave Amanda back in third grade. This was like in the movies.

Hubie just stood there as if his feet had suddenly turned into giant suction cups.

Finally, Ms. Slomonsky noticed him. "Hubie?"

He bolted out the door.

"Hubie, *wait!*"

When he turned the corner he ran into Mr. Bottomly, who was walking in the opposite direction.

"Where's the fire?" Mr. Bottomly roared.

Hubie backed up two steps. "Ah, sorry, Mr. Bottomly." Then he made his escape to the nearest bathroom and locked himself inside the only stall.

His life was one big, rotten disaster after another. Ms. Slomonsky didn't care about him after all. She never had. His ex-best friend squealed on him. Fred was dead—because of him. His number-one enemy was plotting his execution. And to top it all off, he'd probably make a fool of himself in front of everybody this afternoon.

Someone hammered on the door. "Aren't you ever coming out? I gotta go." Hubie reluctantly left his hiding place.

He was trudging down the hall when Marruci shoved him from behind, almost knocking him down. "I'm gonna kill you, *Hu*bert." Marruci swaggered past and into the classroom.

Hubie noticed Frank hauling a pile of books out of his locker. He walked over and stood beside Frank. "I never figured you'd squeal on me."

"What are you talking about?" Frank slammed shut his locker door.

"There's only one way Marruci could have found out about our plan." Hubie stuck an accusing finger in Frank's face. "You told him. *Didn't you?*"

"Hey, you got it wrong. I didn't rat on—"

Hubie spun and headed for the classroom. He wasn't going to stand there and listen to Frank deny he'd done it. Inside, Hubie noticed a circle of girls huddled in a corner of the room. Beth stood in the center with an Atlantic-to-Pacific grin spanning her face. He overheard her say something about a long-distance call from Shelly last night.

This sounded very interesting. Hubie decided to check into it. "I'll straighten the books on the shelf for you, Mrs. Bunce."

She looked up from her desk and nodded.

Hubie began lining up the books as he strained to listen. But all he could make out were bits and pieces. Something about "after baton practice" and "stuck it to Ralph." And then he thought he heard his name mentioned. With all the giggling, it was hard to know for sure. Hubie inched closer.

Beth stopped talking. He looked up from the shelf and saw her staring back at him. The eight-thirty tardy bell scattered everyone to their seats.

One thing about Marruci, he didn't wait long to make his move. Everybody was in the gym locker room changing back into their clothes when Frank hollered, *"Behind you, Hubie!"*

He turned just in time to see Marruci's fist grow larger. Then lights exploded around him.

. . . "Boom Boom came down hard!" The announcer screams into the microphone. "Probably for the last time."

Hubie hears the referee's count. ". . . four, five, six . . ."

Dazed, he looks up and sees Marruci grinning back. Behind him, at ringside, is Lana. Tears caress her cheeks as she calls his name.

"Hubie . . . please get up. It's really you I love.

127

Hubie, *Hubie*—"

The crowd is roaring. "Boom Boom, Boom Boom, Boom Boom . . ."

His head throbs as he slowly pushes himself up. Lana's words echo over and over in his mind. Before Marruci has a chance to strike again, Hubie thrusts his whole body forward. "Eeeoow."

Marruci's face disappears under an avalanche of blows. . . .

"Get this maniac off me!" Marruci screamed as he shielded his face from Hubie's wildly swinging punches.

Even if he tried, Hubie couldn't have stopped. "Who squealed?" he demanded. His arms kept pumping away as if somebody else controlled them. *"Tell me!"*

"Beth. It was Beth. Stop . . . stop," Marruci pleaded.

An arm reached down and, grabbing Hubie, pulled him off Marruci.

"He went nuts, Coach," said Marruci, getting up. "I didn't do anything."

"You started it," Hubie retorted. "I was just protecting myself. And you know it."

The circle of boys grew tighter as they argued

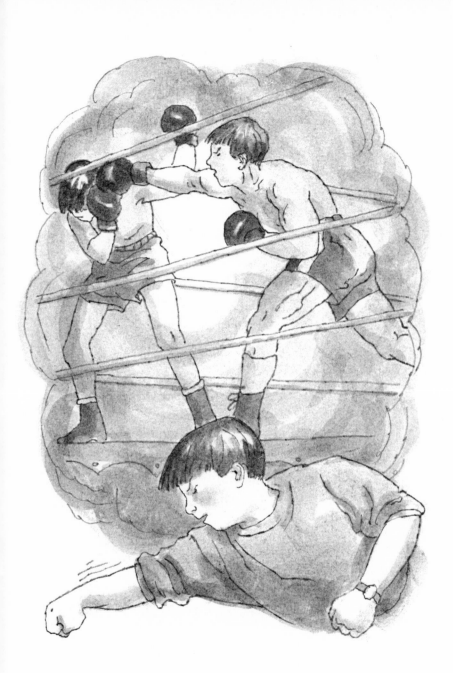

over who started the fight. Frank, leading Hubie's defense, was in the majority.

Finally, Coach held up his hands and ordered everybody to be quiet *now*. Then he added, "We'll settle this in the office."

The boys sat opposite each other outside Mr. Bottomly's door. Marruci, slumped in a chair, didn't look so terrifying anymore.

Hubie rubbed the sore spot on his jaw where Marruci's fist had got him. It was a good hurt. But Fred couldn't look down from where he was and call *Hubie* a chickenhead. Unfortunately, he knew what Dad would say when he found out. Okay, so he hadn't handled it very well. Nothing was settled. But maybe, Hubie thought, there still was time to do the right thing.

Getting up, he walked over and stood beside Marruci. "I . . . I shouldn't have written those notes." He was still standing there when Mr. Bottomly opened the door and told them to step inside.

After a ten-minute lecture on school rules, Mr. Bottomly gave them a stern warning. "Second offenders don't get off easy, so there better not be a next time," he said, looking over his bifocals. "Now get back to your classroom." The boys were leaving when Mr. Bottomly stopped Hubie. "Seems like I've seen your name on a list recently."

Oh-oh. More trouble.

"Now I remember. You're one of the three students speaking this afternoon."

Hubie nodded. That was the last thing he wanted to be reminded of.

"Congratulations," said Mr. Bottomly, pumping Hubie's arm.

Hubie left in a daze. Downstairs, in the cafeteria line, five of the boys in his class patted him on the back and said, "Right on, Hubie." In the lunchroom he saw Frank sitting at the far table near the wall.

Hubie shuffled over and stopped beside Frank. "I . . . ah . . . want you to know that I'm *really* sorry. I should have known you'd never squeal on me."

Frank slid over to give Hubie room to sit down.

"Boy, what a dummy I am," said Hubie, unwrapping a ham-and-cheese sandwich. "I *thought* I saw somebody sneaking around the hall when I planted Marruci's note." He took a bite. "Beth must have figured it all out when Shelly called her last night."

"And then she couldn't wait to tell Marruci.

That was a rotten thing to do." Frank pried the top off a plastic container. "What's this I hear about you speaking at the assembly for the Art Festival?"

Hubie stopped chewing. "I don't even know what I'm going to say." He stared at the half-eaten sandwich. There was no way he could force the rest of it down.

"You're the hero," said Frank, grinning. "You can do or say anything."

Hubie's chin was still sore. Maybe his jaw would lock up when it was time to speak, he thought. He'd heard of delayed reactions before. "Oh, no," Hubie muttered when the bell rang. It was time to go back to the room. The Art Festival assembly started in exactly thirty minutes.

When they got back Mrs. Bunce called him aside. "Mr. Bottomly wants you to go to the stage now. He'll meet you there." Then she gave him one of her approving smiles. The kind she usually saved for kids like Beth Pringle or Rob Halerman.

On the way to the auditorium, Hubie stopped off at the bathroom. After he washed and dried his hands, he stood looking into the mirror. "Ahem . . . It is an honor for me to stand here and take part in this honorable . . . ah . . . Art Festival." That wasn't right. "I . . . ah . . . I'm honored to be part of—"

The door swung open. Hubie quickly took out his comb, took two last swipes and hurried out the door. Onstage, Mr. Bottomly was giving directions. He put Hubie next to Ms. Slomonsky. This was the first time Hubie had seen her since this morning. He wondered if she had heard about his fight with Marruci. He hoped she had. Between his nervous stomach and her presence a mere six inches away, he thought he was going to keel over.

Hubie looked out at the auditorium. Holy Toledo, the place was filling up fast. His heart was pounding so fast, it felt like it was going to burst free from his chest. Then he started to worry about that—he even imagined the headlines in tomorrow's *Post-Journal*: FIFTH GRADER SUFFERS HEART ATTACK ONSTAGE.

Mr. Bottomly got up and welcomed everyone to the first annual Art Festival. While Mr. Bottomly spoke, Hubie tried to think of what he'd say after he began with "I'm honored to be here today." That was too short. Of course, he could start with his full name and the grade he was in. Then what?

"After this brief program, relatives and friends of students will have an opportunity to visit the various art displays throughout the school." Mr. Bottomly cleared his throat. "And now I would like to begin by introducing one of our fine art students here at Samuel G. Love School. Hubert Hartzel."

Why did he have to be the first to speak?

"He is a fifth-grade student in Mrs. Bunce's class."

Oh, no. There went half of his speech. Hubie heard the clapping when he slowly stood up. As every eye focused on him, his knees buckled. He thought he'd never make it to the podium. Somehow he did. But his throat was so dry Hubie wondered if his voice still worked. Turning, he glanced back at Ms. Slomonsky. She was smiling at him. Hubie took a deep breath.

"Ah . . ." His voice echoed in the auditorium. "It's an honor for me to be here today. . . ." Silence. "I . . . ah . . . think the best part about the art program here at Love School is Ms. Slomonsky. This year she taught us things like how to draw in perspective. And sometimes she lets us decide on the kinds of art projects we want to do. I guess that's why it's so much fun."

Hubie paused. He couldn't think of anything more to say.

Mr. Bottomly saved him by going up to the podium. "Thank you, Hubert," he said, clapping. Hubie gratefully walked back to his seat.

While everyone was leaving the auditorium, Ms. Slomonsky came up to him and gave him a hug. "You make teaching art worth it all," she said. Hubie grinned. So maybe she didn't care for him the same way she cared for Coach. But she did think he was a good artist. Wasn't that what really mattered?

He was still grinning as he left the stage for the crowded hallway.

. . ."And now, ladies and gentlemen, I give you the president of the United States." As the band strikes up "Hail to the Chief," the crowd goes wild with applause and cheering.

Slowly making his way to the podium is President Hubert Claude Hartzel. . . .

"Hey, Hubert," called Marruci. Hubie looked up and saw his class, led by Mrs. Bunce, shuffling back to the room. Marruci, at the end of the line, stopped and faced Hubie.

As they stood eyeballing each other, Hubie imag-

ined they were enemy outlaws in an old western shootout.

Finally, Marruci shrugged and turned away.

Raising a pointed finger to his lower lip as if it were a pistol, Hubie blew smoke from the barrel. Then, slowly, he made his way back to the room.